KILLING THE HANGMAN

ELLIE MIDWOOD

The only man who stands in
your own way is you

The RSHA chief and the man, whom Hitler
himself calls The Man with the Iron Heart, arrives
in Prague and soon earns himself a name of *The
Hangman* among its population. When the order
comes from London calling the Czech resistance to
assassinate Reinhard Heydrich, they have to decide
fast, what is stronger: self-preservation or heroic
death in the name of freedom.

Prologue

PRAGUE, Protectorate of Bohemia-Moravia. May 27, 1942

JAN'S HANDS trembled as he was wrapping a highly sensitive bomb, provided by the SOE, into a piece of cloth. Under his long, chestnut bangs, the young Czech's forehead shone with a film of sweat, viscous and transparent – like his fear. His blue eyes, usually so bright and smiling, so wonderfully alert with intelligence, now stared, without seeing, into space, his nostrils flaring as his heart was beating with savage force against his ribcage. The room appeared suddenly devoid of air.

Jozef assured him yesterday when they had just returned from the appointed place, that he – Jozef – would be the one to carry out the assassination.

Jan was there more for moral support – a so-called plan B in case plan A didn't succeed, for reasons which Jan didn't even wish to consider.

But he had nothing to worry about, Jozef patted his cheek in a reassuring manner, pulled him close, by the neck, with his rough fingers, pressing his forehead into Jan's, the usual optimistic grin in place. *Jozef had never had to use a plan B before.*

Jan passed a hand over his forehead with beads of moisture on it, shamefully removing all visible traces of his hesitation, and blew his cheeks out, praying to all the Gods that Jozef was right.

It's not that he wasn't aware of the purpose of the mission that he had signed up for, after all. But back in fog-ridden Britain, in the emerald paradise of Inverness-shire, in their newly established SOE sabotage training camp, everything seemed so much easier than here, in Prague, where he firsthand saw the Gestapo in action. He also saw their chief, the Reich Protector – SS Obergruppenführer Reinhard Heydrich – himself; the man, who Jozef and he had been sent here to assassinate. It was only a few days ago that one of their connections brought the radio message from London, confirming the mission. The rumor was that Heydrich was leaving for Berlin and after that – to France and apparently only Heydrich himself knew if he'd be back in Prague in the foreseeable future. They hastily decided on a date – May 27 – and once again went over the plan; three men waiting for Heydrich's car on the side of the road, which he took every day on his way to work from his residence in Hradčany. The road near one of the streets turned so sharply that Heydrich's Mercedes would have to slow down to an almost walking pace; that's where they positioned themselves day after day, observing and marking everything down, using a bus stop as a convenient excuse for loitering where they shouldn't have been.

It felt like yesterday that Jan saw him for the first time, his intended target. He saw it all again, playing in front of his eyes. *Heydrich – tall, even sitting next to his driver, his face shielded with the shadow of his cap's visor; only the mouth moved into a polite smile when he motions the driver to stop completely to allow an elderly couple to cross the street in front of the Mercedes. They bow their gratitude; the Protector nods with a languid grace and turns away. Jan clenches a gun, concealed in his pocket – Heydrich is hardly four steps away from him; it's impossible to miss from such a short distance. And then, as though sensing Jan's intense stare, Heydrich turns his head and looks him squarely in the eyes, his smile slowly transforming into an arrogant smirk as he shifts his gaze from Jan's hand in his pocket back to his eyes, wide with fear.* Go ahead, boy. Shoot. *Paralyzed with unthinkable terror, Jan swallows hard, moves his lips into a wary smile and, despising himself and his weakness, raises his arm in the Nazi salute. Heydrich doesn't move, only looks down with a barely perceptible air of disappointment and soon turns away entirely as the driver picks up speed.*

Jan never told Jozef about having a gun on him

that day. He never told him that he didn't have the guts to pull the trigger. And now, sitting alone in his room, he wondered if he would be able to pull himself together and carry out the mission or hide behind Jozef's back like a coward – again.

Chapter 1

RASTENBURG. Wolfsschanze – Wolf's Lair – Hitler's Headquarters, September 1941

THE PHONE CONVERSATION, which started out so well, rapidly deteriorated and soon came to a rather abrupt culmination when Reinhard Heydrich slammed down the phone. By some inhuman willpower, he forced himself to contain the fit of rage that was ready to bubble over and spill onto an unsuspecting adjutant. Judging by the latter's frightened look, the idea of being alone in the room together with the infuriated chief of the RSHA, was utterly beyond his desire. Reinhard took a deep calming breath and passed his hand over his blond hair, forcing his emotions under control.

And to think of it, just a few minutes ago he'd walked into this communications room with such a radiant smile on his face, in such a delighted mood, his spirits soaring so marvelously high, and she managed to ruin it all even though she was almost a thousand kilometers away. The scientists declared that the human body possessed over seven trillion nerves, and curiously enough Reinhard found that his "better half," Lina, managed to get on every single one of them. He had just been appointed as the new Reich Protector in Bohemia-Moravia, but even such a remarkable event she managed to twist into something negative, infuriated by the fact that she and the children would have to stay in Berlin at least for a few months until he got settled in Prague. Lina was the first person whom he chose to share the news with and what did he get in response? More accusations of him being "a lousy, ever-absent father" and more screams about her being "the poor neglected wife." It was always about her. The whole world had to stop and cater to Lina von Osten.

I loved her at some point, Reinhard remarked to himself with a sort of cynical curiosity. Now, he was secretly relieved to be rid of her and her nagging, for a few months at least.

"Would you like me to get you some coffee perhaps, Herr Obergruppenführer?" The adjutant's meek voice produced the desired effect; Reinhard even graced the young man with a smile.

"That would be nice. Thank you."

The adjutant saluted sharply and vanished from

the room with commendable efficiency, leaving Reinhard alone with his thoughts.

To hell with her. He finally got what he was after – a ministerial post with direct access to the Führer himself, even Reichsführer Himmler no longer standing between the two. No, he was still grateful to Heinrich for everything he'd done for him. But the truth, which he would never openly admit to anyone, was that the roles between the mentor and his protégé had reversed quite a long time ago, and now it was Reinhard, who was the driving force behind the RSHA and the SD. *Perhaps, first in the Protectorate and then – who knows?* Reinhard's blue eyes gleamed with a hunger that had never ceased to burn inside, propelling him further, higher, consuming everything that stood in his path to becoming what he had always craved; the power to be reckoned with, the power that can decide who is to live and who is to die, the power of God himself.

"My life has to be like this," he proclaimed to his little brother Heinz one sultry August night in the bedroom they shared, tracing his finger from the lowest point near the bed towards the ceiling until he couldn't reach any further.

"And then?" Heinz cocked his head to one side, his soft blond curls soaked with silver moonlight pouring through the open window.

Reinhard didn't know what came after *"then,"* and so, he receded slowly, muttered something with a shade of quiet accusation, climbed out from the constraints of the sheets and padded barefoot to the window to search for answers in the *star-dusted sky. He was only twelve, but he already knew that he would do anything he possibly could to become the strongest, smartest, most feared man in the whole world and then she would never hurt him again. Their mother took some sort of sadistic pleasure in disciplining her sons at the slightest of provocation, with a thick wooden rod across their backs; a year later, the defiant thirteen-year-old Reinhard would tell her off for the first time, sneering with a crooked disdain at her, ugly and panting from her efforts to make him wince at least once. He had long lost his ability to feel the force of her blows, encouraging her instead to add more to the other side – for an even count. She stopped beating him soon after. She started fearing that cold, mocking gaze of his and that inability to feel pain which he had seemed to turn off in himself permanently. Both physical and emotional – for the even count.*

Yes, to hell with Lina, and to hell with his mother; he wouldn't let either ruin his mood. He was the Reich Protector now, with only the Führer above him and he was only thirty-seven years old. His star was shining as brightly as it possibly could and he proved it to his younger self that he indeed made his life follow the trajectory he'd traced before his younger brother that night, who was watching him with the reverence only younger siblings can.

'And then?' Heinz's small voice sounded far too real in his head and Reinhard even shook it to get rid of the unwelcome illusion.

The adjutant walked in with a silver tray, smiling gingerly at his superior.

"I didn't have a chance to congratulate you properly, Herr Obergruppenführer. Please, allow me to express my utmost happiness with your newest appointment. The Führer couldn't have chosen a better candidate for the post than you."

"Thank you," Reinhard murmured and then added in a strangely hollow voice, "what happens to the meteors at the end of their existence?"

The young man paused in his tracks, seemingly puzzled by the unexpected question. "They burn off and turn into cosmic ash, I suppose. But not before they devastate everything in their way."

Reinhard nodded, a faint glow warming his sharp, pale cheeks.

Prague, October 1941

REINHARD HEYDRICH ROSE from his seat at the sight of his new deputy, who had frozen to attention at the door. When an obligatory exchange of salutes was out of the way, Karl Frank hurried over to the imposing desk and gave the proffered hand a firm shake, his eyes searching his superior's nevertheless, as though craving encouragement.

He was shorter than Reinhard; much older, with deep-set brown eyes and harsh lines along his ragged face – a complete opposite of the man now standing across from him. Both appraised each other subtly; Frank – with some greedy fascination and fierce jealousy, Heydrich – with the condescending graciousness of someone with the upper hand. Reinhard suspected that the Secretary of State and chief of police Frank had been very much hoping to get promoted after the Führer decided to remove the "soft" Konstantin von Neurath from the position of acting Protector, but apparently, the Führer had a different view on the matter. The new Protector Heydrich didn't need any hard feelings between himself and his deputy and therefore applied his all to act as his most charming self, which wasn't easy, to begin with, *so Frank had better appreciate the effort.*

Reinhard wasn't a particularly charming man. Ambitious, yes. Hardworking, to the point of obsessiveness; demanding of others but even more so of himself; a perfectionist, who strived to be the best in everything that he applied himself to, be it fencing, music, or managing the Secret Police with an iron fist. His subordinates feared and respected him. His superior, Reichsführer Himmler, nearly worshiped him. Even the Führer himself looked at him with barely concealed admiration. He was a perfect Aryan, an image, from which all of the future generations of Germans would be rubbed off – tall, blond, and ruthless.

"How do you find your new headquarters?" Karl Frank sat in the offered chair and immediately placed a black folder on top of Heydrich's desk.

"Believe it or not, I barely notice the difference between Berlin and Prague," Reinhard confessed with a soft chuckle, already leafing through Frank's fresh report. "All I see for sixteen hours a day – sometimes eighteen or even twenty – is the four walls, my desk, and papers on it. And desks, walls, and papers are all the same everywhere."

"I suppose," Frank conceded, mirroring his superior's grin.

Heydrich was wonderfully arrogant, Frank noted; *and it came to him quite naturally so!* That wonderful arrogance of his lay lightly around him as though a part of a bored monarch's attire. It seemed inconceivable to Frank that, preoccupied with the matters of the state's security, Heydrich didn't notice the fine wainscoting of the room which he currently occupied; the intricate designs on its silky panels; the finest oak, polished to glimmering perfection; the plasterwork adorning high ceilings which belonged in a museum, no less. He noticed everything, all right; he just chose not to acknowledge the fascinating, dazzling beauty of the Czech architecture, preferring the typical, neo-German austerity to it, no doubt.

"The castle is quite remarkable though," Reinhard admitted in passing, scanning the paper with a sharp gaze and marking something on the borders with his pen. Frank straightened a bit in his seat, subtly trying to make out if the notes were positive or negative. "Lina and the children will love it, once they move here. I, unfortunately, only sleep there so I won't have many opportunities to enjoy its beauty, but I still appreciate your offering it to me."

"It was absolutely my pleasure, Herr Protector." Frank dutifully inclined his graying head.

He didn't particularly enjoy bowing to this new master, but he found himself drawn to the new Protector despite his recent resentment. Von Neurath was a weak old man; Heydrich was still very young and sharp like a whip. Frank had already executed over ninety people on his orders, and Heydrich had barely spent three days in Prague as the new Protector. Such fervor, in Frank's eyes, was worth if not admiration, then the recognition, that's for sure. Besides, Heydrich didn't appear to be as such a bad fellow, as many had warned Frank. *Look at him, sitting there, smiling, making jokes even. Not a bad fellow at all.*

"I like what you suggested here." Heydrich startled Frank, slamming the folder shut with a sudden harsh snap and placing his hand on top of it. He had a musician's hands, graceful and white, with long, neatly manicured fingers. Frank quickly took his hands off the desk as though embarrassed by his square fingers and black hair covering the backs of his palms. "But I'm not particularly fond of your methods."

One of the long fingers was now tapping on top of the eagle, engraved in the black leather.

"I apologize, Herr Protector," Frank rushed to lower his head in submission once again, "if my methods appear a bit too harsh; I only assumed that you would prefer swift measures and so I took the liberty of—"

"Too harsh?" Heydrich's voice lifted in surprise before yielding to a short chuckle. "No, by all means, you misunderstood me. I was actually saying that, on the contrary, you are a bit too lenient with the Czechs. If we want to eventually fully Germanize this country, we need to weed out all the alien elements, starting with culture and ending with people carrying the said culture."

"I understand, Herr Protector." Frank hurriedly nodded.

"I want you to entirely eliminate all the non-German elements in the Protectorate's everyday life. No more Czech ethnic music on the radios, in the concert halls, or in the streets. No more national costumes; no former national holidays or celebrations. You seem concerned all of a sudden. What is it?"

"With all due respect, Herr Protector. The people will riot, I'm afraid, if we take it all from them at once, in such a manner."

"But we'll give them free Saturdays instead. Two-day weekends instead of just Sundays off and a lot of new popular German music. German movies. German fashion that will come with German stores. Raise their wages to raise their spirits. Give them some German beer and introduce them to the new German holidays they will love to celebrate. Offer the workers in the factories double rations if they over-complete their quotas. Give them free shoes. Give them unemployment insurance. Raise their pensions. Shall I continue or will you think of something yourself?"

"I will think of something, Herr Protector. I'll prepare a new report for you for tomorrow if you'll allow me."

"Please, do." Heydrich was silent for a moment. Finally, he moved the folder back to Frank, his hand still lingering on its top. "Prague is a beautiful city, isn't it?"

"It is indeed, Herr Protector."

"I don't want to turn it into the capital of the Gestapo terror. I want them to respect me, not hate me. I just want them to understand that I'll be their friend as long as they're mine. As long as they do as I tell them, they will live just as well as people in Germany do. I merely want obedience and discipline, that's all. It's not too much to ask, is it?" He slightly tilted his head to one side.

"Of course, not, Herr Protector."

"I didn't think so. Good. Get to work then, and I'll see you tomorrow."

"Just one more question, if you'll allow, Herr Protector."

"Yes?"

"What about the Jews?"

"You still have Jews left?" Heydrich arched his brow, his expression a mixture of disdain and amusement, before inquiring in a sardonic tone, "was von Neurath working here at all?"

Frank shrugged his shoulders sheepishly in apparent embarrassment for his former superior.

"What of them, your Jews?" Heydrich smiled in a most kind-hearted way and returned to his papers before commenting quietly, "the Führer had selected Prague, Berlin, and Vienna to be the first three major cities to be rendered 'Jew-free.' If that isn't too clear of an instruction, then I'll spell it out in simple terms; *get rid of them.*"

"*Jawohl,* Herr Obergruppenführer. It is perfectly clear now."

"How is the situation with the resistance?"

"It's a process, of course, but it has much improved since your arrival, Herr Protector." Frank inclined his head to one side with a subservient smile.

Of course, it had. City walls were now plastered with countless red posters, from which the names of the condemned communists and other "hostile Czech elements" were spilling onto the streets of Prague, along with their blood in the prison court-yards. Heydrich was more than explicit on their account as well, issuing an order, according to which "hostile Czechs and Poles, as well as communists and other scumbags, must be transferred to a concentration camp for longer periods of time."

Now, he appeared to have decided that it would have been easier to just shoot them all. Or hang them, so as not to waste any bullets on the said "scumbags."

"Good, good. When do you think we'll be rid of the last of them?"

"In a few months, I would think, Herr Protector."

"By summer?"

"*Jawohl, Herr Protector.*"

"Splendid. I won't hold you any longer then. You have a lot of work to do. *Heil Hitler.*"

Chapter 2

CAMUSDARACH IN INVERNESS-SHIRE – SOE sabotage training camp. Great Britain, October 1941

JAN LAY ON HIS BACK, staring into the faded turquoise of the autumn sky with a doomed expression creasing his forehead. The ground pleasantly cooled his body, which felt as though it was on fire after such a marathon. Every single one of his muscles screamed out in pain; lungs, expanding to their maximum with every breath, greedily gulped frigid October air, laced with a salty breeze blowing its relief from the sea. He was training with such stubborn dedication for this test, daily and nightly, when no one would see, creeping into the gym and driving himself into complete exhaustion just to prove to himself – and, what's more important, to his friend Jozef – that he could not only ace that test but outdo him, Jozef, who seemed to always excel at everything. Jan was supposed to be better prepared, after all. A former military man. Taller, stronger, sturdier. And yet it wasn't him but Jozef who once again passed the obstacle course with flying colors. Jan saw his personnel report, too:

Jozef Gabčík — a smart and well-disciplined soldier. Thoroughly reliable and very keen, with plenty of common sense. During the training, he showed himself to be talented, clever and cheerful, even in the most difficult situations. Open, warm-hearted, enterprising and resourceful.

Physical training: very good.

Fieldcraft: good.

Close combat: very good.

Explosives: good 86%.

Communication: very good 12 words/min in Morse code.

Reports: very good.

And in conclusion: *A natural born leader.*

It was that "natural born leader" who was standing over his panting frame now and giving him the warmest, toothy grin.

"I have to watch my back," Jozef offered Jan his outstretched arm to help him get up. "You're treading right on my heels."

"I wish I were," Jan grumbled under his breath and allowed his friend to pull him upward.

He also wished he had a healthy, competitive rivalry with Jozef, like sportsmen do, just to motivate him to do better, to run faster. But Jozef, from the very first day that they met, became not only a close friend but almost a brother figure for Jan; a brother, who was always there, who pushed him when he couldn't push himself any further, who encouraged him when he lost all faith in himself... They were complete opposites. Jan – calm, reserved, and serious; Jozef – the soul of the company; yet, both had more in common than they cared to admit. Both were orphans; no wives, no children, no families to mourn them once they perished from the face of the earth, ravaged by the war and hatred. Both shared the same keen sense of justice which begged to be restored; both weren't afraid to die in the name of it. Well, almost. Jan taught himself to think that he wasn't.

Jozef promised him, with some inexplicable certainty, that their native Czechoslovakia would breathe freely in just a few years and that it would be them, the SOE-trained Czech Resistance fighters, who would make it happen. And Jan, eventually persuaded by his words; caught the contagious bug of the fighting spirit that seemed to never leave his comrade and soon began believing, as well, that all those wonderful predictions would most definitely come true just because Jozef said so. And Jozef was rarely wrong.

It's not that Jan was a coward; quite the contrary. A former military man, he joined the underground in Krakow as soon as the Czechoslovak army was dissolved and even fought in Algiers together with the Free French, and having a *Croix de Guerre* to show for it. Unlike him, Jozef, whom Jan met after running to England, hardly ever spoke about the Czechoslovak Army, to which he also belonged and which had lost its battle before it even began. At first, Jan disliked him immensely; then – looked up to him. Jozef was only a year older than him but what eternal wisdom, what fire burned behind his piercing blue eyes! With him, Jan was ready to go into hell itself if needed.

"Hungry?" Jozef amicably slapped Jan's shoulder, sending a faint cloud of dust flying into the crisp autumn air. No wonder, after crawling on their stomachs for nearly two hours under barbed wire and sand pits, from which they had to shoot at the moving targets. Jozef "killed" all of his; Jan only "injured" three out of five.

"Starving," Jan replied with a grin and passed a dirty, torn hand over his forehead, only now noticing the stinging sensation as the lacerated skin rubbed against the sand, which was stuck to his face. "Damn it. I thought I cut myself while getting out of the 'minefield'."

Jozef only snorted and poked two fingers through the sleeve of his uniform. "Not you alone."

That made Jan feel slightly better. Even though Jozef was still the leader of their group, known to the SOE as Free Czechoslovaks, he was still only a human, Jan reminded himself. Maybe, one day he, Jan, would indeed come first. After all, as Jozef himself always said, *the only man who stands in your way is you.*

They showered and wolfed down their generous meal, then played cards and shared a few beers, also generously supplied by the SOE. It wasn't bad here by any means, but as the evening settled down and the silence grew around them, invisible, unspoken questions began tormenting every single man, it seemed. How many were tortured by the Gestapo butchers while they compared their scratches and bruises received during the training? How many lost their freedom while they were enjoying their game of cards in the safety of their allies? How many died, while they lived?

Invariably, they fell into a dim gloom and welcomed the relief of the lights-out at ten, when they could lie and stare into a black ceiling – as cold and morose as their thoughts.

VILLA BELLASIS, SOE training camp. 26 December 1941

'MY MISSION INVOLVES BEING SENT *to my native country with another number of the Czechoslovak army in order to commit an act of sabotage or of terrorism in a place and according to methods which will depend upon the circumstances that we find there. I will do all that is in my power to obtain the results desired, not only in my native country but also beyond it. I will work with all my heart and soul to be able to successfully complete this mission, for which I have volunteered.'*

"You have to understand that once you sign up for this, there will be no turning back," a stern-looking Colonel moved two identical papers towards Jan and Jozef. "This mission, with which we are entrusting you, is of the utmost historical importance. The assassination of someone of Heydrich's level is unprecedented and unthinkable to the Germans, just like his current policies in our homeland, are to us. We must avenge all of our comrades, executed in cold blood on his orders. We must demonstrate to the Germans that they aren't as invincible as they imagine themselves to be. But as significant as your task is, the risk is even more substantial. We'll drop you over Czechoslovakia and provide you with everything we can in order for the mission to succeed. However, it is of utmost impor-tance that you act as a single, two-men cell without revealing the details of your mission to anyone, including your comrades from the local Resistance. They will provide you with shelter, but that's where the collaboration must end. The stakes are too high to risk exposure, in case someone with such dangerous knowledge falls into the hands of the Gestapo. Once you get a coded go-ahead from London, through a radio operator in Prague, you'll have to rely on your own skill and improvise according to the plan you will have to work out yourselves. And, I have to say this so that my conscience is clear before you two; there is a very slim chance that once you implement whatever plan you agree upon, we'll be able to organize an escape route for you in time. If you manage to escape on your own – good for you. We'll gladly take you back. If not…"

He only pursed his lips in a certain way instead of finishing the sentence.

"Please, do consider this carefully and with an open heart. If you have any doubts, anything at all, tell me now."

Jan wavered for a moment. Jozef calmly signed under the text.

Our death sentences, passed through Jan's mind, for some reason. He hastily chased the thought away and slashed the paper in two with his signature. *So be it. They will die, but not before they send 'The Hangman' to hell, where he belonged.*

They were given only two days to mentally prepare themselves for their mission, which they chose to spend poring over the map of Prague and quizzing each other on the names of the streets and squares until they memorized nearly an entire city by heart. On the eve of the second, the same Colonel loaded them with all sorts of possible ammunition and shook their hands with a solemn look about him.

"You are tasked with a mission of the utmost importance. As you know, Reich Protector Reinhard Heydrich is one of the most powerful men in Nazi Germany as of now. He's efficient in his methods, ruthless, extremely intelligent, and can't be underestimated. A man like him will give you only one chance to kill him; if you don't use it, he'll kill you and it won't be a fast and merciful death. Please, do be careful."

"We will," Jozef assured him with envious confidence.

A British NCO was summoned in, who immediately ordered the Czechs to strip naked, with a typical British coolness. Efficiently and drily, he laid out a choice of clothing before the pair, pointing at each piece of clothing and almost proudly remarking that everything was Czechoslovak-made. Suits, pants, shirts, underwear, matches, toothpaste – *the SOE appeared to have taken everything into account,* Jan remarked to himself with a healthy dose of amusement.

"No need for anyone to find anything remotely reminiscent of England on you, gentlemen," the NCO commented in his characteristic matter-of-fact tone before collecting their belongings and disappearing behind the door.

Instead of dismissing them, the Colonel cleared his throat and began aimlessly searching for something in his papers, stacks and stacks of which littered his desk, together with a military map and their point of destination – a tiny red flag in the middle of nowhere.

"Is there anything else, sir?" Jozef appeared to correctly interpret his superior's fumbling for the latter undoubtedly couldn't bring himself to articulate the right words himself.

Looking at the two uneasily, the Colonel moved two blank sheets of paper towards the Czechs.

"If you would like to make your wills, we still have a couple of hours before the plane takes off." His words tumbled out in a hasty murmur, painful and apologetic.

Jozef stepped forward, dipped the pen in ink without further hesitation and started writing. Jan stepped away, hoping that the gesture would come out natural, as though he was merely giving Jozef space, not trying to desperately work his way out of the room, the walls of which closed in on him like those of a coffin, dark and suffocating. The fire barely crackled in the fireplace, and yet Jan's shirt was damp with sweat. *Some assassin,* he mentally cursed himself.

He quickly jotted down his will that night as well, wondering at how little he appeared to have in this world at his twenty-eight years of age. *'My leather jacket to my brother in Moravia… bicycle to my cousin… Please, look after my family in the event of my death.'* No money, no property, no children to carry his name. Not even a girlfriend to cry over his death. What a sad way to leave this world.

Jozef made a joke about Jan being some friend – *I thought that the bicycle was mine?* Jan chuckled, slapped his shoulder awkwardly, wiped a quick tear from the corner of the eye while no one was looking, crossed out the words that swam before his eyes and added the new ones. 'The bicycle to Josef Gabčík if he's alive at the moment of my passing.' *Now, all better.* They can laugh about it and this means they aren't too afraid. The Colonel heaved a sigh of relief collecting the two papers with only a few lines on them; thought of saying something but changed his mind at the last moment. Just a formal "Good luck to you both" at the Tangmere aerodrome belonging to the secret RAF base in Sussex, and a sharp salute to seal the deal. He would never see them again – alive, that is; he was sure of it.

Jan hid trembling hands under his legs on the heavily laden Halifax, as it was making its slow progress over the Channel, then Occupied France and finally – Nazi Germany, stubbornly navigating its way despite searchlights springing to life here and there and anti-aircraft batteries probing the sky around it and missing it only by some miracle, no doubt.

"Night-fighters," Jozef spoke to no one in particular somewhere over Germany. More bullets whizzing by, more nervous glances among the nine parachutists; two more groups were to be dropped out further along the way for their respective missions. The pilot took to the clouds and lost the fighters – again, by some incredibly lucky chance. Jan was nursing some strange inward hope that

Messerschmitts would just end them all here and now and he wouldn't have to be afraid anymore.

"We can't die tonight," Jozef announced with some owl-like wisdom around him. "Fate wouldn't allow us to die before we complete our mission. Heydrich's appointment as the Protector has perverted the very sense of the word. He's not the Protector; we are. We are coming to restore the correct order of things, how they should be. When the strong protect the weak, not when the strong bully everyone who goes against them into blind submission, or hangs them regardless of age, sex, class or origin. No, we can't die. Otherwise, this whole world won't make sense to me anymore."

Jan nodded but suddenly, as though after Jozef's putting it into words, the whole idea of the assassination appeared almost insane. *Them? Two ordinary men from the Czech Resistance kill the most feared man in all of Europe?* It seemed just as feasible as assassinating Hitler himself. Perhaps, Hitler would prove to be an easier target; in Jan's eyes, Hitler was a madman. Heydrich was an evil genius, a mastermind behind all of Himmler's rabid ideas of the brutal police force and eliminating anyone they proclaimed, "an enemy of the state."

Jan had a nightmare the night before, in which he was shooting at the Reich Protector until there were no more bullets in his gun and Heydrich just stood before him and laughed in his face, that devilish look about his eyes paralyzing him in his place with its glacial, ice-blue fire. Jan woke up, drenched in sweat and couldn't sleep for the rest of the night. *What if they fail? What if Heydrich indeed doesn't die, for whatever stupid, inconceivable reason?* But they were already falling through the very real rabbit hole into the opaque darkness of the night over their native Czechoslovakia and once their feet dove deeply into the snow, there was no turning back. The plane had dissolved into that velvet obscurity as if it had never existed, and only the two silky clouds of their parachutes proved to Jan that he hadn't dreamt it all.

JAN WRESTLED with the parachute which had covered him entirely until he finally untangled himself from its grip. Knee-deep in the snow, he frantically turned his head from one side to the other in a futile attempt to locate his comrade.

"Jozef!" He probed the still, crisp air in a soft voice and then shouted, as the panic started to set in. "Jozef!! Where are you?"

"Scream a little louder; I don't think that our goddamned plane roused enough Gestapo agents around here from their beds!" A gruff voice came from above him.

Only then Jan saw him, caught in the cobweb of branches of a tree; Jozef, busily working his way out of the parachute. Jan laughed in relief, nearly dancing around the tree as Jozef was making his way down, until the latter proclaimed in his usual calm tone, as if the announcement was nothing significant, "I think I broke my ankle. Could you catch me if I jump, so I don't land on my foot and make it worse?"

Of course, he could; he was taller, sturdier, stronger. Yet the Colonel had appointed Jozef as the leader of their small, two-man squad as if sensing some hesitation about Jan and rightfully so. Jan outstretched his arms.

"Go ahead."

Jozef barely weighed anything – slim, wiry, and unafraid of anything.

"Can you walk?"

"I'm going to have to." Jozef circled his arm around Jan's shoulders, carefully probing his way in the snow with his good leg. "I don't think he dropped us in the right place. Did you see the village while we were landing? Right near the graveyard where we are now."

"Yes. I thought it was strange, that he dropped us so close to the populated area."

"Well, the instructions were that he was supposed to drop us near Pilsen, in a forest. Does this look like a forest to you?" Josef suddenly burst into laughter. "And yet, just my luck, I encountered the only tree that stood in the middle of a clearing. Nothing to say this started out well."

"What are we going to do now?" Jan was

already warm from adrenaline, still coursing his body after the jump and from both Jozef's weight and the weight of the ammunition that he carried for the both of them; one backpack in hand, another – slung over his shoulder.

"First of all, get as far away from the village as possible. The probability that they heard the engines of the plane is one hundred percent. Let's hope that they're all good, conscientious Czechs, but if there's at least one pro-German among them…"

Jozef didn't finish. Jan refused to even think what would be then.

"One step at a time now, Jan. From now on, it's one little step at a time."

Chapter 3

WANNSEE, Suburb of Berlin. January 20, 1942

REINHARD CONFIDENTLY NAVIGATED his plane toward the narrow landing strip despite the light snow that had started to fall. Blizzards didn't bother him; on the contrary, he treated the force of nature as one of his opponents, proving to it and to himself, that his skill as a pilot was more than a match for some petty weather conditions. Reichsführer Himmler couldn't stand that trait of his, that almost suicidal desire, at times, to prove himself to no one in particular. Reinhard chuckled under his breath when he recalled the day when his superior wouldn't stop grumbling about Heydrich's escapades in the Fighter Squadron 77, which he had joined in absolute secrecy and without even considering consulting him first. Himmler, the sickly hypochondriac with constant headaches and weak nerves, couldn't tolerate the awful thought of losing his second-in-command, his best man, his protégé, and a good friend.

"I thought you didn't have secrets from me," he muttered, with a shade of offense in his voice, glaring tragically at Reinhard when the latter had informed him of leaving for the front as part of the Luftwaffe, for the first time.

Reinhard only shrugged in response, utterly indifferent and almost bored with Himmler's senti- ments. *You thought wrong, then.*

And then Reinhard's Messerschmitt was hit on the Eastern front; he bailed out behind the enemy lines and Reichsführer nearly had a heart attack at the mere thought of the Chief of the RSHA falling into the hands of the Russians and therefore the NKVD, who would undoubtedly celebrate such an occasion by demonstrating to their German guest their best third-degree interrogation techniques. And Reinhard, meanwhile, wandered around the forest for a couple of days, miraculously managing to escape the feared partisans, together with the Soviet Army; found his way back to the frontline and happily gave himself up to the German patrol. *Name and rank?* They had to be vigilant; Reinhard understood and offered them his name and full title. They exchanged glances, scowled for a few moments until one of them snorted with laughter, slapping his comrade on his shoulder. *Poor fighter ace fellow must have suffered some mighty brain damage to fancy himself the Chief of the Reich Main Security Office!*

Killing the engine of his plane, Reinhard caught himself laughing as he recalled how long their faces had become once they discovered that "the fighter ace fellow" was telling the truth; then stopped at once as soon as two small figures came into the periphery of his vision. A driver and an adjutant; the second, already holding his coat out for him. Reinhard climbed out of the plane, shedding his short pilot's jacket together with his pleasant disposition.

Sometimes it felt like Luftwaffe Captain Reinhard lived and Obergruppenführer Heydrich only played a role in the play that was written by someone else, for someone else. In the Luftwaffe, it was all simple and straightforward; he fought his dogfights, drank cheap wine, played cards with his comrades and shared a good laugh with them over a crude joke. Here, was a different type of work. Here, he was a different Reinhard; invariably stern, brutally efficient, and unforgiving.

Since his return from the front, he found in himself a growing fear of loneliness. Over the years, he had made himself as unapproachable as possible and now, instead of friendly gatherings, he had to dine with men whom he secretly despised. He had broken off all of the family ties with his sister Maria only because her husband was a pathetic drunk and Reinhard didn't want to be associated with anyone of that sort. He barely spoke with his brother Heinz, who made the mistake of expressing certain liberal ideas on a few unfortunate occasions; thoroughly refused to be affected by any of Reinhard's arguments and soon became just a name which his older brother didn't wish to remember.

Captain Reinhard used to have good comrades whose company he genuinely enjoyed; Obergruppenführer Heydrich had subordinates with whom he went into town in the evenings, convincing himself that they were his friends. Eventually, he persuaded himself that it was even better this way. They laughed at his jokes and never expressed unpopular opinions. *That's quite all right,* Reinhard told himself on quite a few particularly lonely occasions, biting down the growing feeling of uneasiness around him. *They always say that it's lonely at the top.* He traded humanity for power, and to him, it was a fair exchange.

Reinhard put his arms through the sleeves of the leather coat that his adjutant held out for him and climbed into the car.

They drove in silence. Reinhard checked his wristwatch; it took exactly fifteen minutes from the small aerodrome to the villa itself, which meant he'd walk through its doors five minutes before the beginning of the meeting. He was not just punctual, he was always five minutes early and God help any person who dared be late for a meeting with him! One time his Gestapo Chief Müller ran into his office, panting and apologizing profusely – *the damned tire blew up!* Reinhard only stared at him silently for a few interminably long moments.

"You have wasted exactly twenty-eight minutes of my time. Twenty-eight minutes, which could have been spent in the interests of the Reich."

From that day on, Müller left his house an hour earlier just in case another accident happened. He didn't mind moping around the office for the whole hour; anything was better than another hard glare and that tone of Heydrich's – a perfect concoction of rage and ice. Reinhard hardly ever yelled; instead, he quietly poured poisonous torrents of abuse in such sarcastic, derogatory terms that two of his adjutants left his office in tears just this month. The third one had been fired two days ago. The fourth one – the fourth one in this January – sat next to the driver, frozen from the wait in the cold and fear, mentally going over all of those things that he had heard about his new boss and praying to all the Gods that he didn't mess up today. The rumors were, Heydrich had sent the third adjutant straight to the Eastern front, whatever the poor fellow had done.

The road, a black ribbon against the pristine whiteness of the countryside, curled its way to the villa – magnificently imposing in its elegant winter attire. The cobbled driveway leading to the entrance was cleared to perfection; Reinhard made a mental note to thank Eichmann for a job well done. He had chosen just the right man as his second-in-command for today's meeting. As soon as Eichmann was appointed as head of Section B4 of the Amt IV – *Jewish affairs* – Reinhard kept commending his extraordinary organizational skills. Well, since they were about to deal with the most significant Jewish issue today, it only seemed appropriate to task him with organizing everything as well.

SS stewards scrambled to attention as soon as Reinhard stepped on the marble of the villa's hallway, which was polished to such perfection that it reflected, with a mirror's precision, everything that came in contact with it. Eichmann was already heading his way, his usual timid smile in place. They exchanged salutes and usual pleasantries while invisible hands relieved Reinhard of his overcoat, cap, and gloves.

"Anyone missing?" Reinhard smoothed his platinum hair despite the fact that not a hair was out of place. He was perfect as always. Irreproachable.

"In my invitation to everyone I indicated that the time of the meeting was at twelve, not at one, to ensure that everyone arrived on time and didn't keep you waiting, Herr Obergruppenführer."

"What am I hearing, Obersturmbannführer? Such deceptive tactics and applied to your own superiors!"

Eichmann blinked, a shadow of uncertainty passing over his face for a fleeting moment before

Reinhard dropped his mask, slapped his shoulder and laughed in the most amicable manner. "I'm only teasing. Commendable efficiency, as always."

"Thank you, Herr Obergruppenführer."

"They weren't too bored with the wait, were they?"

"I kept them busy with some excellent French wine, starters, and cigars, Herr Obergruppenführer."

"Wonderful. Is the stenographer there yet?"

"Yes, Herr Obergruppenführer."

"You know what to do with the records, do you not?"

"Absolutely, Herr Obergruppenführer. Do not worry about a thing; I have everything taken care of."

A smile of pleasure passed over Reinhard's face; at least someone knew what he was doing around here, unlike that horde gathered around the table with appetizers, with their mouths stuffed with lobster and eyes big as saucers, as though they didn't expect his arrival anytime soon. Reinhard waited patiently, in spite of himself, while they were placing the unfinished plates on the perfectly starched tablecloth, to salute him. If they were his subordinates, he would have told them – and not really mincing his words – what he thought about such a reception; however, most of the men gathered here were his equals, if not in power than in rank and therefore he had to swallow his anger and act as pleasantly as possible. He had a written "go" from Reichsmarschall Göring, but the latter made it explicitly clear that in order for this "go" to work, Reinhard needed the support of all of these men. Reinhard forced himself to smile wider.

"I hope I didn't keep you waiting for too long, gentlemen." He only glanced at the closed double doors leading to the meeting room and Eichmann was already pushing them open. "Please, let us not waste any more time and begin. We'll have a little break in about an hour and you'll have a chance to enjoy my new chef's culinary masterpieces. Business first."

The attendees took their respective seats, indicated with small cards with their names written on them. They eyed the folders laid out in front of each and exchanged glances. The stenographer's fingers hovered over the machine, waiting for a sign from Eichmann. The latter nodded – *you can start typing whatever is said; I'll weed out everything unnecessary later.*

Reinhard stole another glance at his watch. *One o'clock exactly. Time to start. Time to change the world.*

"You probably wonder why I gathered you all here today," he began in his usual quiet voice. "You represent different offices, after all: Dr. Luther – Foreign Ministry, Dr. Freisler – Justice, Dr. Schöngarth – Security Police and SD in the General Government, Dr. Lange – Security Police in Latvia, Dr. Stuckart – Interior, Herr Neumann – Four Year

Plan Organization, Herr Kritzinger – Reich Chancellery. We also have here the representatives of the Occupied territories, Dr. Meyer, Dr. Leibbrandt, and Dr. Bühler. Party Chancellery is represented by Herr Klopfer; Herr Hofmann represents the SS Race and Settlement Office. And of course, the RSHA is represented by Gruppenführer Müller, Obersturmbannführer Eichmann, and myself. In case someone present here is not familiar with me, I'm SS Obergruppenführer Reinhard Heydrich, the Chief of the Reich Main Security Office."

The little joke sent the men around the table chuckling. They all knew him, all right.

"I have gathered you here today on Reichsmarschall Göring's direct orders." He paused, letting that sink in. "He had entrusted me and my office with developing what is indicated on the folders that are before you, the Final Solution of the Jewish Question. Dr. Freisler, no notes, please. Everything that we are to discuss here today is not to be recorded in any form except for the official stenography report which will be handled by Obersturmbannführer Eichmann. Also, all the questions after this meeting concerning the problems and methods discussed must be handled with extreme care and only through proper channels, which means through Obersturmbannführer Eichmann to me only. None of your subordinates are to know anything regarding the question which will be discussed today. Is that clear to everyone?"

A soft murmur of reluctant agreement passed over the room.

"The first and foremost purpose of this meeting is to establish clarity on fundamental questions and to coordinate a parallelization of policies, irrespective of geographical boundaries."

Dr. Bühler, Hans Frank's deputy from the General Government of now occupied Poland, raised his hand. Reinhard expected that much; both Frank and Rosenberg had attempted to argue and on quite a few occasions, that they should decide what to do with their Jews and when to do it, which led to countless political conflicts between the SS and the Governors. Reinhard smiled at him before saying in a tone which sounded polite but at the same time didn't particularly inspire the desire to protest, "I'll answer all the questions after the meeting if you don't mind, Dr. Bühler."

Bühler acceded and made a gesture which could only be interpreted as, *by all means, Obergruppenführer. As though I have a choice.*

"In the past years, we have achieved immense progress in our fight against the Jewry. Since 1933, our principal aim was to entirely eliminate all Jewish elements out of political, economic, cultural, and social life. With the help of a number of policies, such as Nuremberg Laws, the Decree of the Elimination of Jews from the Economy, and many more, we successfully purged the Jews out of all of these spheres. With the help of the policy of immigration, between January 1933 and October 1941 – you have exact numbers in your folders, if you please open them – we successfully induced 537,000 Jews to emigrate from Germany, Austria, and the Protectorate."

Someone started clapping; soon, everyone joined in. Reinhard exchanged subtle glances with Eichmann. *So far so good.*

"Yes, we certainly should congratulate ourselves with such immense success. However, with more territories acquired for the future Lebensraum, we are facing a new problem. Ironically, together with new territories, we acquired more Jews as well. Five million from the newly occupied Soviet territories alone."

A pregnant pause followed. Only Neumann clapped his hands in apparent enthusiasm. "Why? It's good for our production, isn't it? Since the outbreak of the war with the Soviet Union, German factories are lacking workforce. Why not make them work? It would be extremely beneficial for the Four Year Plan—"

"No, it wouldn't, Herr Neumann and I'll tell you exactly why. The problem is, the Jews don't particularly like to work." Reinhard flipped the page in his folder and motioned for Neumann to do the same. "Take a look at the statistics from page four, please. Over seventy percent of the latest census; intellectuals, which means that those people haven't held anything heavier than a pen in their hands in their entire lives. And you want to put them in front of the conveyor? I would personally love to see that."

"I wouldn't want them near German factories anyway," Kritzinger chimed in. "They will sabotage the production."

"We have to put them all somewhere!" Dr. Leibbrandt pulled forward. "It's our Occupied Territories that are suffering from this problem the most. Our ghettos are overflowing with them. The epidemics of typhus and dysentery kill our own German guards who are in contact with them; this will just not do!"

"Just do like we did in Riga." Dr. Lange smirked, lighting a cigarette. "Shoot them all."

"Shooting is all fine and well on paper, but in reality, it's one of the worst possible solutions I came across!" Dr. Meyer argued at once. "It does horrible things to the troops' morale! They're soldiers, and these are often women and children there. They have their honor; they don't want to shoot them!"

"They're soldiers; they must obey their superiors' commands."

"What are we even discussing here?! Shooting? Are you even serious?" Dr. Freisler raised his voice in indignation. "Have we in the Ministry of Justice wasted all of these years to come up with the fair, suitable laws just so you would sweep them all under the rug and say, shoot them all? What kind of barbarians are you?! Do you realize what the rest of the civilized world will do when they hear of it?"

"No one will care." Kritzinger shrugged. "Even the Americans turned the ship with Jewish refugees back. No one wants them."

"Even if they don't, such a barbarian tactic will certainly bring the outrage among all of the civilized nations!"

Reinhard was sitting with his arms folded and listening to the arguments, faintly amused. He let them yell and let off their steam for another ten minutes without interrupting until they finally started growing silent and turning their heads to him as if asking for guidance. He knew what to do; they saw it in his eyes, in his sly grin.

Yes, gentlemen. Everything's already taken care of for you. You are only to rely on me, do what I tell you and I'll solve all of your problems, once and for all.

"I suppose you have something to suggest, Herr Obergruppenführer?"

He was waiting for this question, for this perfect silence. Now, he had their undivided attention, their eager, pleading eyes on him.

"Of course. Obersturmbannführer Eichmann and I designed a special program, which will satisfy all of you, I'm sure of it. There will be no more shootings, on a mass scale, that is. No more overcrowded ghettos. No more diseases. Finally, no more Jews," he finished with a soft smile.

"How?"

"If you all agree to the proposed plan and align the policies of your offices with mine, we'll start working immediately. I believe, Obersturmbann-führer Eichmann can explain everything better than I can, since he was the one working all this time in the field, so to speak. Obersturmbannführer?"

"Thank you, Herr Obergruppenführer." Eich-mann nodded. "Recently, we started building a new facility in the concentration camp Auschwitz in the General Government. After a series of tests, including gas vans and lethal injections, we came up with the perfect solution; a cyanide-containing pesticide Zyklon B acts with much better efficiency than carbon monoxide that we have previously used in vans. Only a small dosage is needed to efficiently kill as many as nine hundred people in a matter of twenty minutes. It paralyzes airways and death comes quickly and nearly pain-free. It has already been tested on the Soviet prisoners of war and proved itself most efficient."

"Question." Dr. Meyer raised his hand. "Where do you put nearly one thousand people and how do you make them go there willingly, without causing major panic?"

"Oh, we used the same design that has been previously used during the euthanasia program; a shower room. They go in naked, thinking that they're about to take a shower – no, no, we have shower heads there, pipes, we even hand out soap and towels for them to 'use' – then we close the gas-proof doors and drop the gas through the vents in the ceiling."

"But now you have a thousand corpses on your hands."

"We're installing there crematoriums with industrial-type ovens that can operate 24/7. According to the most optimistic plans, with all of them operating at their full capacity, we'll be able to completely eliminate the Jews in one year. Occupied territories included."

"Will that satisfy the Ministry of Justice?" Reinhard smiled pleasantly at Dr. Freisler who sat through the entire conversation with an extremely sour expression. "No evidence left; therefore, your qualms over the civilized nations condemning us are taken care of. We'll pretend that these Jews never existed. They'll be only too happy to go along with our version."

"I don't believe I was invited here to have any say in this. You have already decided everything. Why all this spectacle?"

"Of course, you have a say in it."

"Do I? Well, I disagree with it. Does my disagreement matter anything to you?"

"It does. What exactly do you disagree with?"

"It's barbaric. Killing an entire race, in cold blood, is barbaric."

"If you can suggest a suitable alternative, I'm open for discussion."

"Sterilize them all. They'll die out on their own,

and this way our generation, even though it will be remembered as paving the way for the Judenfrei Germany, won't be burdened with mass murder."

"Impractical and impossible to implement. What are we to feed them and where are we to keep them, all those years, until they die?"

"Just let them live out their lives where they are."

"Among us? And then, we're back to square one."

Everyone chuckled.

"What do you want me to say?" Freisler made a desperate gesture with his hands. "Do you want to pry the approval out of me like you pry the confessions of the enemies of the state in your Gestapo cellars?!"

A heavy silence fell over the room. Several men shifted uncomfortably in their seats. Müller cleared his throat; Eichmann stole a quick probing glance at Heydrich, expecting a fit of rage to follow.

The latter remained perfectly calm, only his narrowed eyes turned into hard granite. "I don't need your approval, Dr. Freisler. Only your promise to align the policies of the Ministry of Justice with the policies of the RSHA. As long as you do that, you can disapprove of me all you want. The disapproval stopped bothering me after a certain night in 1934."

Kritzinger shot a warning glance in Freisler's direction. *Just keep your mouth shut, why don't you?! They*

say Heydrich shot the Chief of the SA, Ernst Röhm, person-
ally, that night, despite him being Heydrich's son's godfather
and only because he was stupid enough to get into his face
with his SA's superiority, much like you're doing now. Calm
the fuck down and don't piss him off, if you know what's
good for you.

Apparently, Dr. Freisler recalled the Night of
the Long Knives, as well. "The policies of the
Ministry of Justice will be aligned in accordance
with the policies of the RSHA on the Jewish question. You have my word."

"Thank you, doctor. That's all I needed to
hear." Reinhard even smiled in his most charming
way, as Freisler turned away, disgusted with himself
and everyone present. "Anyone else have any
objections?"

Silence. *Thought so.*

"Thank you for your time, gentlemen. And now,
why don't we return to the dining room and raise a
toast to this day – the day, when we changed the
world from the way everyone knew it."

Chapter 4

PROTECTORATE, *February 1942*

JAN WAITED BREATHLESSLY as two uniformed Germans perused his papers with envious thoroughness. Jozef didn't seem bothered in the slightest and even smiled apologetically at the Germans. *Yes, we are both sick, sir. Yes, an ulcer in my duodenum. Yes, hurts like a bitch. Yes, him too. An inflamed gallbladder. We're both on our way to the doctor. Hopefully, he has good news for us; we both can't wait to return to work!*

It was almost a routine by now. With the new Reich Protector came new laws and one of these such laws clearly stated that one had better have a good excuse for loitering in the streets for no apparent reason when one should be working for the glory of the Reich. Jan's and Jozef's papers were in perfect order, stamped by the same doctor who had treated Jozef's foot once they arrived in Prague. Needless to say, the doctor was a faithful member of the Czech Resistance as well.

Jan still couldn't believe that they'd made it this far after landing straight in the field near the grave-yard where they would have been buried very soon, or at least as Jan thought, that fateful night. They quickly buried their parachutes in the snowdrift, stumbled in the dark, leaving traces in the deep snow, making their way to – hell, he wasn't even sure where they were heading since they didn't have the faintest idea where they landed in the first place. There was an abandoned quarry though, a piece of chocolate for each, some meat-extract tablets from their backpacks; two pistols with four magazines and twenty-four cartridges, and two cyanide capsules as insurance. Jan refused to close his eyes until the dawn started to break, leaping to his feet at every sound and aiming his gun at the dusty twilight outside.

There was also a local gamekeeper, who entered their hideout in the morning with a polite cough and a gentle "hello"; there were gamekeeper's friends from the Resistance who just as gently explained to the two SOE agents that they were near Prague and not Pilsen, but they shouldn't worry about their Pilsen contacts now being useless, for they knew just the right people in Prague who would provide them with shelter and all the needed assistance.

Then there was a train station – a Gothic, dark-stoned building with two towers; two backpacks with SOE-provided weapons, pocket knives, some Czech currency, false identity papers, and hopes that they wouldn't be searched. And then there was a Baroque dream of Prague, the headless horseman in Liliova street, the trams with headlights that look like lanterns, the wet snow lining the glistening cobbles, the Moravec family that took them in without any questions asked and then there was the Moravec's neighbor from across the staircase, with her eyes the color of honey and hair the color of gold, with whom Jan fell in love the moment he saw her – *Anna.*

"You ready?" Jozef's voice brought Jan back to reality.

The Germans were already gone; the blizzard receded and turned into a damp mist. The cobble-stoned street was empty.

"Yes."

———

THE MAN WAS tall and collected, with graying hair and a look of an English aristocrat about him – Heydrich's Czech butler. A personal friend of Václav Morávek, the last one of the Three Kings – chiefs of the Czech Resistance. The first King was shot; the second – tortured to death in one of Heydrich's Gestapo cellars. Morávek got away with a severed finger on his hand while escaping the same fate.

The butler didn't introduce himself and outright refused to meet again after this very first encounter.

"Too dangerous. Give me the address of someone you'd trust with your life, and I'll be delivering the information there on my own schedule."

Jozef jotted something down, handed it to the butler. Jan stole a quick glance at it and saw a name, *Libena Fafek*. He wondered if it was the same Libena who met them at the train station in Prague and took them to the doctor. Jan thought that Jozef was looking at her in a certain way; he was right then.

"Tell us about him," Jozef inquired blankly, not wasting any time on pointless pleasantries.

The butler took a long drag on his cigarette. "What do you want to know?"

"You live with him under the same roof. What is he like?"

The butler was silent for a moment. After a pause, he started speaking, his words slowly gathering conviction. "He works a lot. Spends a great deal of time in his study, even on weekends. He's secretive. Always closes the door when he makes a call no one should be listening to. Keeps all his papers in a safe; his desk is always empty when the maid goes in to clean it. He likes to ride his horse. Enjoys his violin and plays it very well. Tries to spend as much time as he can with his children on weekends. He adores his little daughter, Silke." A subtle smile warmed his face. "I was surprised, to be honest. I didn't think he was capable of any human sentiments. But yes, he adores his little girl. Whatever was left of a human in him, is thanks to her."

It was strange hearing such an odd conclusion, *whatever is left of a human.* Maybe that was the reason why their British handlers gave such an appropriate name to the operation – *Anthropoid* – "human-like," but not a human after all. Jan stopped toying with a box of matches he was holding and lifted his eyes at the butler. "What is his schedule like?"

"Oh, he's obsessively punctual. You can check your watch by him. Comes and goes at the same exact time every day, almost always alone, hardly ever with an escort."

"That's very careless of him," Jozef noted.

"Not careless," the butler corrected him. "Arrogant. He likes to think that after beheading almost the entire Czech Resistance in a few short months, he can ride around the city not only without an escort but in an open car, as well. It's almost as though he dares someone to attempt something. But don't underestimate him. If you make one mistake and one mistake only, he'll see to it personally that you won't see the light of the day for the rest of your very few and very painful hours." He paused and added, "Morávek says, it was him who shot one of the Kings after the latter refused to speak. Unlike some bureaucrats of his kind, he's very much capable of killing. His hand won't waver, don't even count on that."

"Does he have any weaknesses?" Jan asked.

A resolute shake of the head was his reply. "No."

"A mistress in the city he likes to visit?" Jozef pressed.

"No. Whatever he does, he does in Berlin or Paris when he goes there. He even made a speech recently before his SS men to that effect; 'do whatever you like within the four walls of your own home or the officers' mess but make sure no Czech sees you do it. We must give them an example of self-control and order. The Slavs must know that we are the masters here and we have no weaknesses,' and everything else to that effect. He's quite fond of making speeches lately; I must tell you. Bores his subordinates with them to no end. He already imagines himself the master of the whole occupied East, no less. He even bought a globe, to match the one that stands in the Führer's Reich Chancellery, he bragged. I wonder if that's where he's aiming eventually."

"The Chancellery?" Jan raised his brow.

"No. In the Führer's place," the butler replied calmly. "He was drinking one evening with two of his comrades and quite explicitly told them that he 'wouldn't think twice about finishing the old man off if he gives him any shit.' Pardon the language, I was merely quoting."

Jozef whistled. "What happened to the famous SS loyalty and following the Führer unto death?"

"Reinhard Heydrich has loyalty to one man only and that man is Reinhard Heydrich." The butler checked his wristwatch and rose from the bench. "My break is over. I must go back. It was a pleasure knowing you young fellows. I wish you the best of luck. Do not try to contact me, please; I have a family here in Prague. If you need anything, ask through Libena."

"Thank you for your help." Jozef shook the man's hand firmly.

The butler only nodded stiffly and quickly disappeared into the whitewashed February day.

Suburbs between Panenské Brežany and Hradčany

Anna's laughter, so carefree and wonderfully melodic, made Jan's breath catch in his throat, choking him up with the romantic joy of having her so near. With her lithe, graceful frame perched on the frame of his bicycle – her bicycle, actually, which she had generously offered him since he needed it more than she did – she held onto his hands as he was pedaling unmercifully fast down the cobbled street. Past the church and its scornful stone gargoyles following their progress with their bulging eyes, past the university closed down for an indefinite time due to the new policy of Germanization, past the post office and the statue of some king – Jan still didn't know Prague too well, to the very outskirts of the city and onto the wide road leading up to the very lair of the Blond Beast.

"Be careful; there's a very sharp curve further down the road, in Holešovice Street!"

He only laughed in response to Anna's warning, too sure of himself; too diligent in his desire to impress her; too in love with those fine gilded threads of her hair flying into his face with every new gust of wind, caressing his cheeks like the softest cloud of radiant dust dripping with sunlight…

"Jan!"

He tried to stop as soon as he realized that the turn – almost a hairpin – was indeed far too sharp for him to skillfully glide into it at the speed that he was going and on an icy road at that. Jan swerved around a man, who cursed him out and narrowly escaped the seemingly inevitable collision with the tram, the shrill sound of its bell adding to the man's cursing. Catching his breath on the sidewalk, he held Anna tight in his embrace, his bright eyes fixed on her with a nearly awed expression, tragically apologetic and wonderfully blue.

"Are you all right?"

"I am, but you did give me some fright!" She play-swatted him on his arm as her raspberry lips curved into a smile despite her resolute desire to keep a stern face. "I told you there was a sharp turn there!"

"I thought you were exaggerating," he admitted, embarrassed and adorably flushed.

"No." Anna moved the stray lock away from his forehead. "My uncle owns a car and he has to move at walking speed while taking this bend when he drives to the countryside. Too busy here – a bus stop, tram lines, people running across the street all the time. If you ride too fast, you can easily kill someone by accident. Or kill yourself, if you crash into a tram. The turn is deadly."

"Deadly, you say," Jan muttered, looking around with a strangely agitated look about him.

"Why, yes. But now you know better and hopefully won't do any such crazy stunts anymore."

"This is the place," Jan whispered excitedly, his eyes gleaming. "It's perfect."

The following morning, using a bus stop as an excuse to loiter on the street, Jan and Jozef smoked in silence, subtly observing the road, the turn, the trams' comings and goings and the people hurrying to work. Jan didn't know why he even brought the gun with him – *just in case,* he thought to himself. Anna confirmed that Heydrich's driver took this exact road – *he had to; it's the only road that leads to his residence* – but she wasn't sure about the timeframe.

"The butler said, Heydrich's an early bird,"

Jozef remarked as though reading Jan's preoccupied mind. "Maybe, if we're lucky…"

After the church bell across the street from the alchemist's shop struck nine, Jozef started glancing at his watch with more concern. The working crowd, so conveniently whirling and shifting around them before, had dissolved into the bright opalescent day, leaving the two men alone and exposed in the middle of the deserted street. A Czech police patrol, curiously resembling English Bobbies in their round helmets, passed by, thoroughly pretending not to notice the suspicious couple. Jan voiced the idea of going home. Jozef argued that they should wait for five more minutes, stubborn as ever.

"Our police may be cutting us some slack but we certainly don't need any more Germans checking our documents," Jan pleaded with him, gently pulling on his sleeve. "They will start recognizing us soon, with the rate at which they have been inspecting our papers lately."

"Wait just a few more moments. He'll be here; I can feel it."

"Jozef, let's go!"

"You go if you like. I need to see him."

"Why today?"

"I need to see him," Jozef only repeated with an obstinate look which Jan loathed at times.

And then it glided towards them; triangle, bright-red flags first, a small silver Mercedes sign, long black body polished to an onyx perfection, and the glass blinding them with the reflection of the sunbeams. Jozef's hand froze within a centimeter of his lips, the forgotten cigarette's tip slowly turning into ash as he stared, wide-eyed, with his mouth slightly ajar. Next to him, leaden with fear, Jan held his breath against his will, his hand clasped tightly around the gun concealed in his pocket. The car crawled unhurriedly; the driver raised his gloved hand to shield his eyes from the sun and slowed even more as an elderly couple appeared on the road. The man next to him, his face half hidden with the rich fur collar of his overcoat and his eyes covered with the shadow of the visor of his cap, motioned for the driver to halt. *Let them through. I'm feeling generous today.*

Jan stared at him without blinking. Reich Protector Heydrich was within a few steps of him, his arm resting leisurely on the edge of the door. Jan's hand on top of the gun began to tremble. Heydrich turned his head to him, a faint, mocking smile playing on his lips as he slid his glance lazily over Jan's frozen frame and fixed his gaze on Jan's pocket.

He knew; Jan could swear.

Their eyes met. With beads of sweat racing along his back despite the cold temperatures outside, Jan slowly moved his hand out of his pocket – shamefully empty and still faintly trembling – and raised it in the Nazi salute. Heydrich's mouth curled in exquisite, cruel disdain. He turned away, arrogant and full of contempt for the Czech. *Disappointed*, flashed in Jan's mind.

The black Mercedes was long gone when Jozef murmured quietly next to him, "I should have brought a gun with me today. I had the most profound conviction that I'd see him. And the car was just standing there; did you see it? If only I had a gun on me!"

Jan swallowed with difficulty, red with shame.

"I liked that joke you pulled, with the salute." Jozef had already seized Jan's arm and was walking him along the tram tracks, laughing, completely oblivious to the latter's distressed state. "Very befitting, ha-ha!"

Jan's smile came out more like a grimace. He was trying his best not to break down.

Chapter 5

PRAGUE, March 1942

Reinhard traced his fingers on top of the soot-smeared frame of the Soviet tank, carefully concealing a hunter's triumph in his gaze. The beast, brought to Prague from the Eastern front, was good and dead. It would never bare its teeth anymore and that's precisely how Reinhard preferred such Eastern beasts.

"What crude work," he muttered, reaching into his pocket to extract a perfectly white handkerchief to wipe the invisible Soviet dirt off his hand.

Karl Frank, his loyal deputy who followed him like a dark shadow, promptly inclined his head in agreement. "As with everything in the Soviet Union, Herr Obergruppenführer."

"Exactly." Reinhard slowly circled the brightly-lit hall with his gaze. "And that's precisely why we went through all these pains with this exhibition. I want to show not only the German people but my Czechs as well, what *Das Sowjet Paradies* really is, so that they appreciate more the luck they have, living under the protection of the Reich and not like those Eastern animals in the Soviet Union. Paradise indeed."

"This exhibition was a brilliant idea, Herr Obergruppenführer," Frank agreed emphatically. "Did I hear it correctly that Minister Goebbels himself expressed his desire to display all this in Germany as well?"

With a twitch of a conceited grin, Reinhard bit on his lip to prevent himself from smiling openly. "You did hear it right. I thought of sending him a bill for doing his work for him. Propaganda is supposed to be his domain and here I am, doing yet another office's job. As if I didn't have enough on my plate already."

He walked around the silent hall with Frank on his heels; touched Soviet guns, so utterly unsophisticated in design but so astonishingly deadly. Stood in front of the Soviet Yak plane with a veritable hole in its fuselage; stared at it long and hard. It was a similar Yak that had ended his days in the Luftwaffe. Little Yak that, according to Reichsmarschall Göring, was, by all means, no match to his highly praised Messerschmitts. Reinhard flew a Messerschmitt that day and a lot of good it did. The crudely-made Russian plane turned out to be much lighter and maneuvered with such ease that Reinhard couldn't even catch him in his crosshairs despite the supposed superiority of the German machine. And then, to add injury to the insult, the degenerate Russian pilot tricked him with such ease into following him towards the Soviet frontline that Reinhard only realized his mistake when a burst of gunfire shoved through the metal of his plane. Having waved his wings in gratitude to the anti-aircraft battery on the ground, the Yak was gone. Reinhard was falling behind the enemy lines, still not believing such a humiliating turn of events.

"Such simplicity. Primitivism even," Frank's voice behind his back distracted Reinhard from his musings.

Reinhard nodded curtly and turned away from the offending Yak. "Indeed. Primitivism. They will never win a war against us."

Reinhard thoroughly ignored the gnawing memory pestering him like a pesky fly. *They were a superior species, the Germans. And what happened there, with the Yak, was a stupid mistake, that's all. Just like the setback with Moscow. They'd take it eventually.* Reinhard almost persuaded himself that he believed his own words.

An exhibition worker appeared from behind the closed doors, leading to the small auditorium. "We're ready with the film, Herr Obergruppen-führer. If you would please follow me."

He was already holding the door open for the

two men. Reinhard proceeded into the darkened hall made into a temporary movie theater for the duration of the exhibition, welcoming the distraction. He had asked the SS war correspondent in his charge to film specific things and hopefully the fellow, who came highly recommended, didn't miss out anything.

It turned out, he didn't. As a matter of fact, he followed Reinhard's instructions with envious thoroughness, finding (God only knew where!) such filth and derangement that even Reinhard found himself pursing his lips in disgust on quite a few occasions as the film rolled.

"How can they live like that?" Frank muttered next to him, making a vague gesture of amazement with his arm.

"They don't have to suffer for too long," Reinhard promised with a confident grin. "As soon as we colonize the lands and give them to our farmers and workers, all this degradation will be wiped completely off the face of the earth. Together with the people, who carry it."

No, the voice behind the scenes didn't say any of that, of course. Instead, it spoke with great compassion of the Russian people's plight as pictures of burned churches, primitive dwellings, diseased children with flies crawling on their bodies and even faces, and starved peasants, changed one after another.

Oh, the relief with which they welcomed the

German soldiers! – *That was filmed in the Western Ukraine,* the war correspondent fellow commented quietly. They couldn't find any relieved-looking people in Russia itself, no matter how hard they tried; only the partisans who shot at them at the slightest of provocations and hanged them in droves regardless of their rank or position. Reinhard waved the comment off; *no one would know the difference anyway.*

More destroyed Soviet tanks lined the field as the camera moved further, following the German advance. Reinhard tried not to think that in place of each destroyed one, ten new ones would appear before the German troops the next day. The factories, producing them, had been wisely moved behind the Urals right after the German invasion.

"The Urals will be our Eastern border."

Reinhard only realized that he spoke out loud when Frank addressed him. "Their armament factories—"

"Their armament factories will be all destroyed by then."

"Of course, Herr Obergruppenführer."

The propaganda film came out to be an absolute perfection – even Reinhard himself couldn't have made it better. He thoroughly shook the correspondent's hand and congratulated him on his success.

The refreshments and a light lunch were already waiting for them in a separate room. Forgetting his steaming coffee in a delicate china cup, Reinhard occupied himself leafing through the propaganda booklet that would be distributed for all the guests attending the exhibition the following day.

"I could swear that the last time you submitted it to me for my approval, it was almost fifty pages long." His sharp gaze met Frank's as Reinhard turned the booklet towards his deputy, his index finger pointing at the last page's number – 43.

"You are correct, as always, Herr Obergruppen-führer. It used to be forty-eight pages long," Frank replied, carefully avoiding his superior's inquisitive look.

"What happened to the five missing pages?"

"Nothing. I took the liberty of removing them out of the booklet. They were irrelevant to its contents."

Reinhard regarded Frank with infinite, mocking patience as the latter squirmed in his seat, seemingly in the hope that *Herr Protector* would just leave the whole matter alone.

"Is there any chance I can see the booklet that I have approved? Or have you destroyed them all already?" he asked, at length.

"No, of course not, Herr Obergruppenführer." Frank rose from his seat somewhat tiredly, as though admitting his defeat. *Herr Protector* never left matters alone, so the hope was in vain. He should have known better. He also should have known that having a photographic memory, *Herr Protector* hardly ever forgot things, even such trivial ones as the number of pages in a damned booklet.

Frank left his superior to enjoy his Czech beer, to which he had acquired quite a taste recently and soon returned with the original booklet. Reinhard even obliged him with a smile. Frank by now knew better than to expect anything less than a reprimand following such cunning, unnatural smiles.

"And why exactly did you take the GPU part out?" Heydrich finally asked, shuffling through the last five pages.

Frank looked at him, almost with accusation. *Do I really have to spell it out? With your phenomenal memory, you must remember exactly what's in that section. Too close to home, if you ask me. That's why I took it out. But I can't quite tell you that and not anger you; can I?*

Instead of bringing arguments in his defense, Frank simply took the booklet out of Heydrich's hands and started reading. "The brutal terror Bolshevism exercises through the GPU is perhaps the best answer to the frequent question of why the Bolshevists fight so bitterly at the front. Twenty-five years of terror have produced a gray and broken mass who silently follow orders because that is their only way to remain alive. Resistance means death, often the death of the entire family. The bestial terror regime of the Jewish GPU is best seen in the sadistic methods of torture used against supposed 'enemies'."

He paused, looked at Heydrich again. *Blood fault law and the way we wipe out families in our dungeons? Ring any bells yet?*

The Reich Protector remained unmoved, with the same half-a-smile sitting slyly on his face. *Why did you stop? By all means, continue.*

Frank did. "According to a captured commissar, nearly 5,000 people were shot by the GPU in five years behind the dungeon's iron bars. The cell is tiled. The condemned were brought to the cell and shot in the back of the neck. The corpses were moved to the side and sprayed with a hose to wash away the blood. A fan provided fresh air so that the next victim would not faint from the blood, because he was to remain conscious until the last moment. Another narrow cell was used to secure confessions. Prisoners were forced to kneel for hours. If they stood up, they hit the ceiling and set off an alarm, when a spotlight would be then aimed at them. If they sat on the small seat, they got an electric shock that forced them off. A wooden prong on the door pressed against their stomachs."

Frank shot Heydrich another long look.

The latter chuckled quietly to some thought of his. "An interesting invention, a room like that, is it not? Do you think we can organize something similar here, in Prague?"

"I'm sure it's easily done, Herr Obergrup-penführer."

"Well, continue. What's next?"

"The worst of all terror institutes of the GPU is the forced labor camps in which millions of innocent victims die every year. Only rarely do they know why they were taken from their families and jobs to work in the icy wastes of Vorkuta or any of the numerous other labor camps. Most of them are there only because free labor was needed somewhere in the wilderness. No one cared about them. They were shipped there under the principle; 'people? We have enough of such trash.'

"The unhappy victims, condemned with or without cause, follow a miserable path from which death is the only real escape. It begins with a spy, often a member of one's own family. One night the GPU knocks on the door and takes its victim. Put in narrow cells, worn out by endless interrogations, and finally forced to confess by the usual methods of torture, with or without a verdict, they are transported to forced labor camps with inadequate food, often in the bitter cold. Many die on the way. In the forced labor camps themselves, they are stuffed into small barracks. The pitiful food ration depends on the amount of work done. It is never enough and the hard work soon leads to exhaustion. The smallest offense is punished severely by a spell in an ice cell. Continual overwork, bad food, and the lack of sanitary facilities soon lead to serious illness. The sick, forced laborers, are put on starvation rations to speed their deaths, for the GPU has no interest in weak workers. They must be disposed of as quickly as possible.

"Very few forced laborers return to freedom. Kajetan Klug was one of them. He was a leader of the Marxist Defense League in Linz. After the unsuccessful insurrection of February 1934, he had to flee the revenge of the Dollfuss regime. His route led him through Czechoslovakia to the land of his dreams, the 'Paradise of Farmers and Workers.' In Moscow, he took over the leadership of the Austrian immigrants and became a party member. But he soon learned the misery of the workers and farmers. When he openly criticized these conditions, he was accused of espionage. He was arrested, tortured, acquitted, and finally condemned, with no proof, to five years of forced labor in Central Asia. The wintry wasteland of Vorkuta finally opened his eyes to the real nature of the 'Paradise of Farmers and Workers.' A few days before the beginning of the war with the Soviet Union, he succeeded in escaping to the German embassy. Along with the embassy personnel, he was able to reach Germany."

Reinhard burst out laughing. "So he did. And we sent him to Dachau on the very same charge that the Russians sent him to Vorkuta for – espionage. I still remember the case quite well. The irony of it, eh? That poor fellow!"

A sharp look replaced an unexpected laughing

fit at once. "You still didn't tell me why you took the GPU section out of the booklet."

Frank took a deep breath, carefully selecting words. "Because unlike everything else listed in this booklet, the GPU section is…"

His voice trailed off despite his attempt to keep it firm. Heydrich was watching him like a hawk.

"…the GPU section is?"

"The GPU section is… It can easily be called 'the RSHA section,' Herr Obergruppenführer. Pardon my straightforwardness," Frank finished, with a bravery that he had never expected of himself.

"And?"

Much to his surprise, Heydrich didn't burst into a rage fit but on the contrary, remained positively calm. Smiling even. For some reason, that smile of his unnerved Frank more than the shouts that he had expected to hear.

"And… People can draw parallels."

"What people? Who knows about what we do behind closed doors? Who knows about our cellars besides us and our deputies who know better than to talk about such things? Who knows about the camps? Who knows about torture?" He shrugged with a dismissive look and sipped some more of his beer. "You're wrong about one thing, my dear Frank; unlike our Soviet counterparts, we know better than to let our enemies of the state walk free. No one will escape our camps. No one will tell the rest of the world what happens in our cells. And when we're finished with all this scum, there will be no need for those camps, those cells and dungeons, for there will be no more scum to fill them with. Please, distribute the original booklet, with the GPU section included, Frank. Our people need to see them as monsters and us – as saviors, for we really are their saviors. They just don't see the whole picture yet. They will never need to learn about it. They will only praise us once we're done. And those people currently in our custody? As your wonderful booklet wisely noted, 'we have enough of such trash.' No one will miss them."

PRAGUE. *March 20, 1942*

REINHARD STOOD over the corpse of a man, studying the gunshot wound in his temple. *A shame.*

"He shot himself before we could… We did our best to capture him alive, Herr Obergruppen-führer," a quiet voice with a barely detectable tremor in it, whispered behind his back.

"And look at how successful your operation turned out." Sarcasm dripping out of every word, Reinhard only clasped his hands behind his back, tighter.

Colonel Morávek. The last of the Three Kings.

The last acting head of the Czech Resistance, dead; lying pale and waxy at his feet. Reinhard turned his head with the tip of his boot. *Talk about a late birthday present.*

He won. He beheaded the Czech Resistance. He was the ultimate predator in the food chain; yet, all he could taste on the tip of his tongue was a bitter disappointment.

"The things he could have told us..." Reinhard murmured in spite of himself with a tone of desolate finality in his voice.

His agent cleared his throat behind his back. "People don't always talk."

Reinhard turned sharply on his heels to face the man. *Eastern front! Penal battalion!* His eyes perfectly expressed his sentiments before he even opened his mouth.

The agent quickly produced a stack of notes before his superior, with a reverence of a mere mortal in his effort to appease an angered, ancient God, with a timely sacrifice. "But their pockets do just fine. It appears he carried nearly all of his documentation on his person when heading to the meeting we had set up for him. Through this, we have managed to uncover the identity of an Abwehr agent, alias A54, who has been working in Czechoslovakia this whole time. We're already raking the city in search of him."

Reinhard took the news silently. Stood, staring

at the corpse for a few more moments, deep in his brooding, then turned away at last.

"Try to get at least that one alive, will you?" he threw over his shoulder, heading over to his open car.

Chapter 6

PRAGUE. May 1942

JAN SAT on Jozef's bed, his unseeing gaze fixed on
the opposite wall, as his friend was pacing the room
in front of him, agitated and flushed. They had just
received a coded message from London. According
to the latest intelligence, Heydrich was said to be
leaving for Berlin soon, and after that – to France,
and permanently. It appeared that Hitler, inspired
by Heydrich's exemplary dealing with the Czech
Resistance, decided to offer him a new posting,
where he would just as effectively deal with the
French Resistance.

"Was that all in vain then?" Jan whispered
quietly, searching Jozef's face.

Jozef stopped his pacing in an abrupt manner.
"Of course, not!"

"But he's leaving in a few days…"

"It only means that we have a few days to carry out the plan." Jozef shrugged, as though stating the obvious.

Jan licked his parched lips, a feverish gleam shining in his blue eyes. "But we're not ready—"

"Not ready?" Jozef cried and closed his eyes, forcing himself to calm down before continuing in a much milder voice. "We're more than ready, Jan. We've been preparing for this for months. We found the perfect spot. We have been monitoring his movements through his butler this whole time; we know his routine better than ever."

"Routine? What routine?" Jan whisper-yelled back in a very, unusually for him, restless excitement. "We only know the timing of his comings and goings, yes. But as for the escort? He mostly travels alone; that's true. But what about those times when he traveled with an armored car full of the SS on his tail?"

"What about them?" Jozef's tone was so decidedly nonchalant that Jan stared at him in disbelief.

"*What about them?* They'll stuff us with lead before we know what hit us!"

"So, they will." Another unconcerned shrug followed. "Jan, listen to what I tell you. I know that you don't want to die. Neither do I, believe me. I want to kill that Hangman, make it back to Britain a hero, maybe go on a few more operations, and then, when the war is over, I want to come back to my native Czechoslovakia, marry Libena and have many beautiful children with her. I do want that, very much. I know that there's a chance that this will happen. But I also know that there's a bigger chance that it won't. Before we set out on this mission, the Colonel told us that we would be on our own after carrying out the mission. If we do make it out of the country – good. If we don't, we don't. But we must carry out what was entrusted to us, all of these sentiments and arguments aside. We can't just dismiss the few months of work by saying, *oh well, he's leaving, what bad luck. Maybe the French will be more successful.* I don't know about you, but I won't be able to look at myself in the mirror if I let him go, Jan."

Jan rubbed his forehead with both hands before muttering so quietly that Jozef barely heard him, "I know. Me too."

"Are you still up to it then?" Jozef searched Jan's features, creased with anxious lines. "If you aren't, tell me now. We know a couple of men from our group that was dropped from the same Halifax as us in December. I can use Karel Čurda instead. He knows about the operation anyway, I'll just have to fill him in with the details and—"

"Čurda is an unreliable drunk!" Jan protested immediately. "Don't you remember how he once blurted out that he admired Hitler back on the base in Britain? Was it not you, who made a report on him to the Colonel?"

"And Colonel spoke to him and found no threat in his actions. Čurda does love his drink, but he's an alright man. He's been working with the rest of the group here in Prague for a few months now. They say, he's a likable fellow and does a good job."

"I said, no. Why are we even talking about it? I said I'd do it and I will. Or is it you? Do you doubt me, is that what it is? You think I won't have the guts to go through with this?"

Jozef shook his head with a sad smile. "Of course, not. I know that you will die along with me if needed. I just... *don't want you to.*"

Jan's eyes stared with a question in them.

"You love life much more than I do. You love your Anna and you don't want for it all to end so abruptly. And I don't want this for you. That's the only reason why I offered—"

"Jozef, I'll do it." Jan caught his hand and gave it a reassuring pressure. "We came here together and we'll leave together. You're right; I don't want to die. But I would never abandon you. I'm ready."

"You sure?"

"I've never been so certain in my life."

Jan smiled at Jozef in spite of himself. He had almost persuaded himself that he was speaking the truth.

THE FOLLOWING day dawned hazy and pale-pink.

They decided to act fast, escort or no escort and to hell with the consequences. They went out with Anna and Libena the night before and danced with them, desperately trying not to think that those could quite possibly be the last few hours they shared together. They drank, but very little. They savored every bite of their dinner with the hunger of condemned men. They parted their ways, heading in two different directions; Jozef with Libena on his arm, and Jan – with Anna. The night was so full of life, so full of promise, and they almost forgot about death hovering over their heads. *That day, Reinhard Heydrich went to the opera,* Libena mentioned in passing during the dinner. Everyone fell silent.

In the morning, having whispered his goodbyes to Anna, Jan sat on his bed for a very long time, his fingers grasping at its edge. He washed his face, moving like an automaton. Shaved. Brushed his hair. Got dressed. Made sure that the jacket allowed enough space for the ammunition.

Yet, Jan's hands trembled as he was wrapping the highly sensitive bomb, provided by the SOE, into a piece of cloth. Under his long, chestnut bangs, the young Czech's forehead shone with a film of sweat, viscous and transparent – like his fear. His blue eyes, usually so bright and smiling, so wonderfully alert with intelligence, now stared without seeing into space, his nostrils flaring as his heart was beating with savage force against his ribcage. The room appeared suddenly devoid of air.

Jozef assured him yesterday when they had just returned from the appointed place, that he – Jozef – would be the one to carry out the assassination. Jan was there more for moral support – a so-called plan B in case plan A didn't succeed for reasons which Jan didn't even wish to consider.

But he had nothing to worry about, Jozef patted his cheek in a reassuring manner, pulled him close, by the neck, with his rough fingers, and pressed his forehead into Jan's, the usual optimistic grin in place. *Jozef had never had to use a plan B before.*

Jan passed a hand over his forehead with beads of moisture on it, shamefully removing all visible traces of his hesitation and blew his cheeks out, praying to all the Gods that Jozef was right.

Urgent knocking on the door made him nearly jump in his place. It was only Jozef.

"Ready?"

Jan nodded, demonstrating the bomb.

Jozef opened his long raincoat and produced a Sten submachine gun, disassembled in two smaller parts to fit along the side of his arm. The third man, Valčík, their lookout fellow who was supposed to give them a signal once he spotted the car, was shifting his weight anxiously from one foot to another behind Jozef's back. The Moravec family – a husband who never asked any unnecessary questions, a wife who cooked the best dinners in Prague and whom the Czechs affectionately called "aunt," and their young son Ata who openly admired the two mysterious guests who hid guns in their pockets – they all waited in the hallway, big-eyed and solemn.

They shook hands with the husband; hugged the wife warmly; tousled Ata's hair.

"Don't worry." The boy gave Jozef a toothy grin. "I remember what you said about the crate."

The parents exchanged confused glances, but Jan smiled sadly, recalling what his comrade told Ata just a few days ago. "See that crate, where your mother keeps her apples? The Germans can beat it until it starts speaking. But you, you must not say a word when they ask you anything at all. You understand? Not a single word."

Jozef squeezed the boy's shoulder tightly before rushing out of the door. No time for goodbyes today. No time for tears or useless sentiments. The man, whom they were about to kill, was a formidable foe and they couldn't afford a mistake. And so, they picked up their heavy suitcases, left the apartment and walked toward the tram stop without a single look back.

The ride was tense, interminable. Jozef stood rigidly near the door, his arm long and immobile on his right side, concealing the deadly weapon. Jan's eyes peered greedily into the streets flashing behind the glass, imprinting them into his memory. *Not too many German patrols today, good. Not too hot today either, so Jozef's raincoat shouldn't attract any unwanted attention.*

Jan glanced at his comrade again. The latter seemed to be deep in his brooding. *Was he thinking about Heydrich?* Jan wondered. Jan sure was.

Jan could picture him in all his vividness having his breakfast while leafing through a newspaper, or a report perhaps. The butler did say that he was obsessed with his work, didn't he? So, perhaps he was reading some report right now and his wife was reproaching him for not paying attention to what she was saying about the garden. Perhaps he nodded absentmindedly, muttered something to get her off his back and only put down the papers (or the newspaper?) when his little daughter Silke distracted him with some mischief. She was Heydrich's favorite child – again, according to the butler – and Heydrich never reprimanded her for anything, which was not the case with Silke's two brothers. She was allowed to run into his study when he was busy talking to a subordinate, climb onto his lap and demand her kiss. Perhaps, she was sitting on her father's lap right now, hugging him by the neck and asking him if he would take her for a ride on his horse that evening after he came back from work.

Jan shook his head in a vain attempt to clear it. The strangest thing was, how much he had learned about his target, to the point where he started seeing him as a human and not… someone who's not. *Anthropoid.*

"He loves his daughter and plays his violin so beautifully that it makes tears spring to one's eyes," the butler told him.

Jan wished he didn't. Jan didn't want to see the human in him, didn't want to kill *the human.* He wanted to kill the monster, *The Hangman,* and less than anything, did he wish to imagine him hugging his little daughter, now.

"Are you coming?" Jozef's voice woke him up from his daydreaming.

His comrade chuckled at Jan's confused look and motioned his head towards the stop. The tram slowed down and they got off.

"Talk to me, Jozef."

"About what?"

"About anything. I want to talk. I don't want to think."

"All right. Have you heard the legend about St. Wenceslas' crown which is kept together with the Keys of the City, in St. Vitus Cathedral?"

"No."

"The legend says that whoever wrongfully places the crown on his head will die within a year, along with his eldest son."

"And?"

Jozef's eyes sparkled with mischief. "And they say, Heydrich couldn't resist the temptation and tried it on the day President Hácha presented to him the keys to the city, when Heydrich was first appointed as the Reich Protector."

"Who says that?"

"People. No one knows for sure, but it makes a nice story, doesn't it?"

Jan grinned, following his friend into the darkness of the house's hallway. "Do you suppose it's true?"

Jozef paused before the door and shrugged with the same smile before knocking. "I suppose, we'll soon find out."

They picked up their bicycles from their connection and set off on their way past Gothic cathedrals; past German patrols with their hobnailed boots clinking on the cobbles; past storefronts advertising a pure Aryan business with the words *Čisté árijské obchod* and cafés with signs in both German and Czech; past a crude graffiti on a wall: *'Židi ven'* – 'Jews, get out' – inevitably approaching their destination – Holešovice Street. Valčík was already there; they exchanged handshakes, quiet remarks, and headed their separate ways – as it had been agreed. It was today, or never. That evening, Heydrich was supposed to fly out to Berlin, perhaps to never return to his little Czech Kingdom, of which he spoke with such fondness and disdain, all at the same time.

Jan watched Jozef stroll toward the tram stop and take his seat on the bench, his right arm, with the raincoat wrapped around it, resting casually on his lap. Jan watched Valčík head toward the hill, from which he would signal them with the help of a small mirror, alerting them to the approaching car. Jan watched the hustle and bustle of the city around them, feeling strangely detached from its grotesque reality as the clock, which had just struck nine on top of the tower, was writing history where the fates of the four men were so closely intertwined. *Any minute now.*

But minutes passed and the signal didn't come. *Half past nine now* and Jan caught Jozef's nervous shifting in the bench. A sickening feeling of a déjà-vu started overwhelming Jan, reminding him of the day when they waited for the black Mercedes to appear on the road at the same exact spot. That day, Heydrich was also uncharacteristically late. That day, Jan saw him for the first time. That day, he had a chance to kill him and he couldn't force himself to.

Jan started counting pigeons in front of him, just not to think, just not to go mad from all this tension that was straining his nerves to the point of nearly breaking. Then he began counting V's, adorning the walls, passing trams, posters and even the ground, drawn with a small child's hand and purposely not removed by a diligent German one. The Germans stole the symbol from the Czech Resistance like they stole the country itself from the Czechs, and appropriated the proud symbol like they appropriated its factories and people.

Quarter to ten. The street was nearly empty now, only two very suspicious men loitering there without any seemingly good purpose. It only took one "conscientious citizen" to point them out to the nearest patrol and they were as good as dead. Jan's grip on the cloth that cradled the bomb inside his pocket tightened against his will.

The clock struck ten. *He wasn't coming.*

Jan threw a desperate glare at Jozef, but his comrade stubbornly refused to meet it. He continued to expect Heydrich with a sort of humiliating and obstinate sense of hope, like an abandoned lover who refuses to admit the painful truth of being stood up for a date. Jozef stared at the top of the hill with such intensity in his gaze as though appealing to everything that was holy and watching over his country, not to disappoint him.

He wasn't coming. Perhaps, he had decided not to go to work at all today and go straight to the airfield, where his plane was waiting for him. Perhaps, he was already on his way to Berlin and they were so very late…

And then, a blinding light caused Jan to raise his hand and shield himself from it. Jozef sprung to his feet, invigorated, anxious, alert, and ready. The signal came and along with it – a sickening mixture of adrenaline, fear, and hope, which made Jan painfully aware of his wildly beating heart.

Jan moved closer to the road as well; cursed at the sight of a tram which was rolling unhurriedly their way, its bell chiming at the worst possible moment. The car would appear any second now and it would block it, and then—

Jan bit his lip as the black, polished body of the car slowly crawled around the bend. Held his breath as Jozef walked across the rails, extracted the Sten submachine gun from under his raincoat and directed it straight at the two men, sitting in it.

The driver hit the brakes.

Nothing happened.

His breath coming out in hectic gasps, Jan stared, his eyes wide open in horror, as Jozef hit the Sten, aimed it again and again but no shots followed. How many times did Jan hear his fellow SOE agents curse the damned thing that was good for nothing and either shot on the slightest of provocations or jammed at the worst possible of moments and refused to shoot at all!

And Heydrich was already rising to his feet, getting his gun out with a deadly determination on his face and aiming it at Jozef's terrified face.

The bomb! Some invisible voice shouted inside Jan's head. His fingers curled around it pulled it out of his pocket as both Heydrich and the driver was busy shooting at his comrade, who was making his hasty escape, using a tram as a convenient shield from the German bullets. His heart nearly breaking his ribcage with its savage force, Jan stepped forward and threw the bomb at the car, watching its movement as though hypnotized. The driver jumped out, following Jozef who had disappeared behind the tram, mere seconds before the explosion blasted through the street.

The force of the explosion made the windows in the tram burst and shower the street with their opalescent, icy torrent. The Mercedes lifted in the air and landed heavily onto the cobbled road, emanating the acrid smell of burnt tires. As though mesmerized, Jan watched an SS jacket, which had been carefully laid out by Heydrich's maid, onto the back seat – cleaned and perfectly pressed – for him to change into, before his flying out to Berlin, fly up in the air and slowly make its way onto the tram lines. Only then Jan forced himself to shift his gaze back to the car.

Jan stood, rooted to his spot, as his intended target got out of the front seat, holding his side but with the gun firmly squeezed in his hand. *Of course, they didn't kill him. What were they hoping for? He wasn't a man, after all; at least that part their commanders, who gave such a befitting name to the operation, were right about.* Only as the gunshot whizzed past his ear, did Jan burst into a run, further from that beast as they had rightfully called him, propelled forward by sheer instinct of survival. One thought only pounded in his frantic mind; *they had failed and The Hangman would surely kill them now.*

Chapter 7

REINHARD KEPT SHOOTING until the gun started producing only empty clicking noises in his hand. He proudly noted how steady his arm was. He proudly noted that he didn't feel any pain, despite blood slipping through his fingers, staining his gray uniform. He started laughing even, softly at first and then louder, finding it particularly hilarious. *Pathetic Czechs! They thought they could kill him. Him, Reinhard Heydrich whom they appropriately gave the name of Young Evil God of Death. Didn't they realize that Gods couldn't be killed?*

But then he suddenly couldn't feel his legs anymore and sank to the ground, very much surprised by such a betrayal caused to him by his own body. Now, sharp, searing pain was there as well, together with the realization of his own mortality. His driver Klein was already kneeling next to him, muttering something unintelligible.

"Get that swine!" Reinhard yelled at him, pointing with his hand, with the gun still clasped tightly in it, in the direction in which one of the assassins disappeared.

Klein took off running, his shots sending the crowd, gathered around the tram, scrambling and screaming. Reinhard remained on the ground, supporting himself on his elbow, refusing to lie down despite the agony slowly radiating from the torn flesh in his back.

The street came into focus before his eyes, slowly, deliberately, frighteningly real. Alarmed faces, shouts, panic; the shimmer of the broken glass around him became tangible, mortifying. A woman appeared out of nowhere. *Is Herr Protector all right? Does he need help? She'll fetch someone at once* – a blonde, German angel, God bless her. He watched her stop the car and argue with two men in its front seat, who kept throwing glances his way, none too thrilled with the idea of aiding their Protector. *Fucking Czechs*, Reinhard cursed to himself, *should have lined them all against the wall from the very beginning...*

The blonde was already pulling a confused driver out of another car – a Tatra van. He, too, was trying to protest something, but this time she would hear nothing of it.

"He'll help you into the car, Herr Protector," the blonde spoke to Reinhard with a reassuring smile.

Reluctantly, Reinhard allowed the Czech to help him to his feet, before growling, "I'll walk myself," and nearly fell again if the Czech hadn't caught him in time.

Reinhard hated him with all his might at that moment. Hated the feeling of being helpless – for the first time in so many years; hated the gawking crowd around him; hated seeing his car with its rear blown up; hated the Czech's hands on him as he helped him into the front seat.

"My briefcase," Reinhard told the blonde, motioning to his car.

She promptly ran up to it, fetched his briefcase and arranged it on his lap.

"Are you comfortable?" She asked, looking over his tall frame cramped into a much-too-small passenger seat, with concern.

"No," he admitted after a moment's considera-tion. "I want to lie down in the back."

The blonde was back to arguing with the driver in Czech as Reinhard felt more blood dripping through his fingers. He said nothing, just clenched his jaw tighter, pale and proud.

"He says, the van is full of shoe polish he deliv-ers. It smells there."

"I don't care, just let me lie down."

The blonde and the Czech helped him into the back of the van, where he lay on his stomach, one hand still clutching the gun on top of the briefcase that the blonde brought along. In the crook of his other arm, he carefully hid his face, twisted with pain and bitter disbelief. That was not how this was all supposed to end. He was much too young, much too strong, much too powerful to die now, killed by some fucking Czechs, in the back of a shoe polish delivery van. As the van finally started making its way towards the hospital, Reinhard bit into his sleeve, fighting the dizziness off. He wouldn't die if he stayed alert. He wouldn't die. He wouldn't let them win.

In the hospital, there were more wide-eyed Czechs. Reinhard lost count of the number of times he asked for a German doctor to be sent in – they didn't understand him. A young nurse took him to the operating room, helped him onto the table, removed his bloodied jacket, shirt, paused briefly staring at his half-undressed frame for a few seconds, muttered something in her incomprehensible language and ran off, leaving Reinhard to his devices.

"Oh, for fuck's sake!" He cursed out the nurse and her modesty; the damned bitch must have gone to fetch a male doctor to help him remove the rest of his clothes. At the rate this was going, he would die before they took pains to at least bandage him.

Much to his relief, two doctors appeared, at last, one of them German. Reinhard breathed through the pain as they examined his wound, his teeth clenched so tightly that he could hear them grind when yet another painful jab of pincers probed his torn flesh. The German explained that they needed to do an X-Ray. Reinhard scornfully refused the help and stood before the machine even though he was half-expecting his body to collapse any second now. Out of some inhuman willpower, he made it this far, still conscious, still standing before the damned machine, with a broken rib, perforated diaphragm, his thoracic cage damaged, and a piece of shrapnel lodged in his spleen. The German doctor was already saying something about an urgent operation; Reinhard shook his head, ghostly-white and stubborn as ever, demanding the best surgeon from Berlin to be flown in.

"The time is crucial, Herr Protector," the doctor insisted.

Reinhard saw his face swim in front of his eyes. *Fuck, so it was.*

"Will I die if you don't operate?"

"It is a possibility."

"Can you at least summon the best specialist you have in Prague?"

"Of course, Herr Protector."

Reinhard allowed him to take him back to the operating room, and only there he closed his eyes.

THE SS GUARD opened the door, letting Frank in. Reinhard forced himself to raise his head from the pillow, searched his subordinate's face for any clues.

Frank smiled brightly and gave him his usual crisp salute. Only the stench of his cigarettes betrayed his state he so thoroughly tried to conceal. He must have been chain-smoking again, trying to calm his nerves.

Reinhard made an effort to part his lips. "Is it me or the Führer?"

"I beg your pardon, Herr Obergruppenführer?" Frank tilted his head to one side.

"You were smoking so much... because of me or the Führer? You informed him, didn't you?"

Only a little over an hour had passed since the operation. Reinhard was still a bit dazed, but at least they provided him with enough morphine to numb the pain.

"I did, Herr Gruppenführer." Frank lowered his eyes.

"Let me guess; he threw one of his rage fits, didn't he?" A sneer twisted Reinhard's mouth.

Frank concealed a quiet chortle. "He ordered to fly the best doctors for you from Berlin. They'll make sure that the local ones did a good job."

"What else?"

"He demands to shoot ten thousand Czechs in retribution."

"Typical." Reinhard closed his eyes, leaning back into the pillow. "And what about me?"

Frank fumbled with something in his pocket, thoroughly escaping his superior's gaze.

"You can tell me. It's all right."

"He said, it was an idiotic thing that you did, driving in that open car like that. He said, that how could a man of your importance be so cretinous enough to be guilty of such self-neglect and something else to that effect. I apologize; those were his exact words."

Reinhard appeared to be amused, much to Frank's surprise. Or relief, if he were completely honest with himself.

"What of those two? Did you catch them yet?"

"I took the liberty of summoning the forces of the SS, the SD, the NSKK, the Gestapo, the Kripo, and three Wehrmacht battalions, in addition to the local police forces, which were already at our disposal. Overall, more than twenty thousand men are taking part in the operation. All the roads are blocked. The city is virtually sealed. We'll find them, Herr Protector. You can rely on me."

Reinhard nodded. Frank was his best man. He would get those two from under the pits of hell if needed. Reinhard could sleep soundly.

Chapter 8

THE CHURCH of St. Charles Borromeo. Prague, May 1942

JAN LEAPED to his feet once the connection brought the man down the steep steps leading to the crypt in which they had been hiding. He was the last one, whom the parachutists were missing from their small company – Jan's best friend, Jozef Gabčík. They hadn't seen each other since that fateful morning; neither had they any news of each other's whereabouts. Jan stayed with Anna that sleepless night after the assassination; the night, spent in hushed whispers, interlaced fingers, and heart-wrenching what-ifs. He ran first thing in the morning, as soon as the curfew was no longer in effect.

All civilians, without exception, are forbidden to go out on the streets between 9:00 p.m. on May 27 and 6:00 a.m.

on May 28 – Jan still remembered how his hands trembled when he heard the same message being repeated on the radio every ten minutes. Jan ran on May 28 at 7:30, armed with what was left of their British ammunition and a sheer hope that he would make it to the church, to which the concierge – a resistance member and one of their connections – took him. The sympathetic priest showed him down to the crypt, concealed beneath the altar. The Gestapo were dangerously close on their heels.

"They usually don't search churches," the priest reassured him with a warm, fatherly smile. "So, you and your friends will stay put here until everything calms down."

"There's no way to take you out of the city; not now anyway," the concierge added, passing Jan his canvas backpack, the metal clinking of the SOE goods in it soothing the latter's shattered nerves. "All the roads and railroads are closed. Forests are being tightly monitored. Dogs everywhere. Better not risk it. So, you sit tight and I'll try and fetch the rest of your comrades. No need for any of you to risk being discovered by those leather coats. They're out for blood if I do say so myself. Arrest people without any rhyme and reason."

"Any news of Jozef?"

"Not yet." He squeezed Jan's shoulder. "But don't fret. I'll find him."

He did; only Jozef wouldn't stop blaming

himself for the failure and apologizing to everyone, who would listen and to Jan in particular.

"He was right there, in front of me! I could see the markings on his jacket, that's how close he was! If only that piece-of-trash Sten didn't jam…"

At those words, which he repeated with the obstinacy of a broken record, Jozef would drop his head into his hands and shake it, bitter disappointment creasing his features.

"It's not your fault," Jan would console him gently.

"Of course it is. I failed you, and I failed the mission." Jozef's head would shoot up, his eyes staring brightly with fire burning in them. "But you! You're the one who the true hero is! How timely you threw that bomb! And you injured him!"

"What good is it? It was a scratch, and he didn't seem to even notice it." Jan would purse his mouth into a thin, resolute line.

"You did what no man thought possible. You injured him, Jan. You showed them that he's not some fearsome creature that is impossible to kill but a man made of flesh and bones just like us, mere mortals. And even if he'll be back to work, in a couple of weeks, people will keep thinking about it and who knows? Maybe planning; and maybe, acting. Inspired by you, Jan. You did a wonderful thing there, my friend. A truly wonderful, historical thing; you just don't realize it yet."

It stormed that night. A cold moon floated

through the ominous clouds, full of charged energy. The lightning split the skies in two, waking the men in the crypt with its silver, dazzling light. Jan couldn't sleep. He stared out of the small barred window, positioned at the very ceiling, into the violent night, his mind just as turbulent and disturbed as the downpours, drenching the uniformed men outside as though wishing to drown them all, once and for all. They stood, silent and wary; their soaking wet uniforms weighing them down, as the news started to spread with the first morning hours, dawning on them with its petrifying brutality. The old prophecy turned out to be true. The usurper, who had wrongfully placed St. Wenceslas' crown on his head, did die – precisely nine months after doing so. Some of them, perhaps, indeed believed that. Some, perhaps, shrugged it off, proclaimed flatly that Czech doctors were at fault and crushed a finished cigarette under their iron-lined heel.

"Septicemia, I heard."

"No, the bomb parts were poisoned; I learned from a reliable source but don't repeat this."

Heydrich did die, and the mission was a success, but Jozef was right; Jan didn't realize it.

No, Jan didn't realize anything, except for the fact that the crypt was pressing him down with its oppressing stone as the blurred days slipped by, bright blue and restless; that the barking of police dogs wouldn't let him sleep at night; and that, despite The Hangman being dead, some village had been just entirely wiped out in retaliation because someone decided that its population was somehow complicit in the assassination.

"Lidice," one of their fellow parachutists muttered and shook his head with an expression of a desolate finality. "I told you that the whole assassination was a rotten idea. So many people dead, for nothing."

Jan cried quietly in the corner. Jozef chain-smoked next to him. "Don't listen to him. It wasn't for nothing."

"But for what, Jozef?" Jan sobbed. "For what? Someone else will be appointed to his position and the terror will continue. And those innocent people! Their blood is on our hands, don't you see?"

"You killed him, Jan," Jozef only repeated as though in a trance, a smile transfixed on his unshaven face. "You're a hero. Your name will go down in history."

"At what price?" Jan whispered with intense gravity and hid his wet face in his arms, folded over his lap.

Even Anna who brought them parcels with food every other day didn't seem to distract him from his brooding. Even her words about the Germans, announcing an amnesty to anyone, who would come forward with information regarding the assassins within five days, didn't seem to raise Jan's spirits.

"They announced it two days ago. It appears that they have no more leads to the investigation and this is their last chance. They hope that someone will come forward but no one will; I just know it!" Anna beamed her beautiful smile at the parachutists. "Three more days and this all will end, and we'll find a way to get you out of the country."

A hopeful murmur passed through the crypt.

Anna's hand found Jan's. "I'll go with you if you want. You said it yourself that couples attract less attention."

Jan kissed her fingers one by one and nodded, even though fresh tears still shone in his eyes.

"Libena will come tomorrow with food." Anna turned to Jozef before leaving. "We're taking turns, so it's not too conspicuous. For now, she asked to give you this." A pack of cigarettes found its way into Jozef's grateful hands. "She said, you probably smoked all of yours already."

"She knows me too well." Jozef chuckled, fondling the gift in his hands, embarrassed but positively beaming.

"Three more days," Anna promised.

But something went wrong.

JAN COULD NEVER GET USED to sleeping down in the crypt. It felt as though it was suffocating him – a stone-lined tomb where, by an ironic twist of fate, living people now spent their nights instead of dead saints. Despite his comrades' reservations, every evening he made it up the stairs, through the hidden entrance behind the altar and onto the second floor of the church. He slept right there, near the balustrade, with his jacket as his pillow and his submachine gun resting by his side – just in case. Jozef also started coming up, together with him; bored or restless without the man who had become like a brother to him in the course of the past few months, but he invariably followed Jan wherever the latter went.

That night, it was them two who heard someone knocking on the church's door. It was them, who saw the SS Stormtroopers hit Father Petrek across the face and force him inside. It was them, who immediately opened fire, showering the unwelcome guests with torrents of lead. It was them, who alerted their comrades in the crypt that their game was up.

Clearly not expecting such a violent greeting, the Germans quickly disappeared behind the doors, dragging their injured to the safety of the street.

"There must be hundreds of them outside," mumbled Father Petrek, stunned from the blow but otherwise unharmed, as soon as the two parachutists rushed downstairs to check on him.

Jan exchanged glances with Jozef. *So, it begins then.*

"Watch the entrance," Jozef immediately

assumed the commanding role and ran to the altar, shouting to the men inside the crypt to come up and bring all of the ammunition they had.

In less than five minutes, a silence had befallen the church once again. All seven Czechs waited in their assigned positions; three on the balustrade, another two – on the round staircase; Jan and Jozef – behind the altar, their machine guns trained on the entrance. *Let them come in. We'll show them such hospitability, they will curse the day they were born.*

The Germans on the other side of the front door seemed to be pondering their next step. The Czechs patiently waited, their fingers resting on the triggers. They had enough ammunition to last them for hours and they knew well enough to spend it wisely, to shoot rapidly, aiming to kill as many as they could, until the last bullet was spent.

At that point, they all knew that they would die here, but the same resolution burned in every man's eyes; to take as many Germans with him, as was humanly possible.

The door creaked open. The men's grips tightened on their weapons, eyes staring steadily. The SS Stormtroopers opened fire prior to pouring inside – twenty or thirty of them, no less – and Jan grinned crookedly at such a stupid strategy. Almost half of them were gunned down from above within seconds; the second half gathered their wits and pulled out, slamming the door shut after themselves. This time, they didn't even bother with their injured who now littered the floor, moaning in pain.

Valčík finished them off one by one from the top of the balustrade. No need for any SS hero to collect his submachine gun and fire at one of the Czechs, with his last breath.

Minutes dragged, taunting and straining everyone's nerves. What an interminable wait; what insufferable silence! Jozef licked his lips next to Jan. *The poor devil must have been craving Libena's cigarettes,* Jan thought with a sad smile.

The SS commander (or at least Jan assumed it was him) was shouting something at his men outside – the scenario which had repeated itself quite a few times in the course of the next couple of hours. The SS commander shouted, his troops poured in, died in tens, and took cover without as much as injuring any of the Czechs.

The dawn started to break. The Germans got quiet once again. The Czechs checked their cartridges – enough to take on at least the same amount as they already had. The Germans seemed to be rethinking their strategy.

"Give yourselves up!" A familiar young voice sounded from behind the tightly shot door, riddled with bullet holes. "You will be treated as prisoners of war like we were. The German command guarantees it…"

Jozef's eyes shone with anger. *Fucking bastards! Using the boy like that…*

"Was it Ata?" Jan whispered, hoping so desperately to be mistaken.

"Yes."

"So, the Moravec family is arrested then?"

"Judging by the fact that it's him speaking, the parents are both dead," Jozef's voice came out deadly dull.

Jan swallowed a sudden lump in his throat. *First Lidice, now this?* More blood on their hands and this time it was much more painful, much more personal, much closer to home... If the family hadn't taken them in, they would still have been alive. An ordinary family, who merely couldn't stand and watch their country go down the drain – dead, because of them.

Jan suddenly wished for all of this to be over, for he wasn't sure that he would be able to live with this guilt for the rest of his life. *What are you waiting for? Come in; finish us all. I am so ready to go...*

The SS troops obliged, but this time they were smarter; they started hurling grenades inside and, covered by the acrid smoke, snaked their way along the pews and threw a few to the balustrade before Jan and Jozef could gun them down.

Once again, the silence. Jozef called out to his comrades on top; only two voices out of five responded. The metal clinking of the hobnailed boots was nearing again. They were getting bolder, more confident. Jan was shooting without stopping, but he could already see the tops of their steel helmets creeping up, stepping over their dead comrades on top of the balustrade, no doubt, congratulating themselves on their first success.

Rapid fire from the opposite side quickly put an end to their celebratory mood. Their green-gray clad bodies joined the ghastly carpet of their comrades, already lining the marble floor of the church.

"Take cover!" Valčík shouted from the top. "We'll hold them as long as we can."

Jan and Jozef hesitated.

"Go now and stay down!" Valčík screamed again. "They don't know how many of us are here. Maybe, you'll make it out of here alive; please, lads, do stay alive and tell them how we showed those Nazi pigs what's what!"

Jozef quickly pushed the altar to the side and opened the trap door, leading to the crypt.

"Come Jan. He's right. The SS don't know about the crypt. They don't know our exact number. And if we do make it out of here alive, I promise you here and now, I'll go on as many operations with you as possible. I'll volunteer for every single one, to avenge them all."

Jan threw a last glance at the balustrade and dived into the cool underbelly of the church. The priest rushed to abandon his cover behind the pew to move the altar back in place.

JAN LISTENED to the muffled voices coming from the church and still hoped for something, still believed in Jozef's optimistic declarations about the future feats that lay ahead of them. He couldn't possibly know that at the same exact moment Karel Čurda, their fellow SOE commando who once got drunk and blurted out his admiration for Hitler on the base, was standing above the dead bodies of his comrades, laid out in front of the church, and was naming them to his new German masters. He took them up on their offer of the amnesty and the money which they had offered as a bonus and didn't even flinch at the sight of his former SOE comrades, bloodied and broken, being dragged outside with the first rays of the sun. He smoked German cigarettes and shook his head negatively when Karl Frank demanded if that was all.

"Two more," he replied through the interpreter. "Gabčík and Kubiš. They must be hiding somewhere in the church."

Jan couldn't know that both Anna and Libena were interrogated in one of the Gestapo cellars while Frank was giving the order to turn the church upside down to find the missing parachutists. Jan couldn't know that Anna came the day before instead of Libena because Libena went to the doctor, who told her that she was expecting Jozef's child.

Jan couldn't know that in the morning a Soviet tank troop wrote the name *"Lidice"* along the length of their tank turrets and were fighting their battle, in the name of it. Neither did he know that Reichs-führer Himmler was sitting at his desk at that very moment and staring at the angelic smile of the post-humous mask that he had ordered to be taken from Heydrich's face and wondering what he was going to do now after he had lost his best man, his idol whom he had secretly admired, the man without whom this whole SD would fall apart like a house of cards.

Jan only knew that he was still alive and had his best friend at his side and that together they did the unthinkable, something that would never be forgotten, something that he had never expected of himself. And that would suffice for the moment.

Afterword

Thank you for reading "Killing the Hangman"! Even though this novella is a work of fiction, most of it is based on true events. If you have any questions concerning the authenticity of certain events or characters or would like to proceed with further reading, feel free to connect with the author via Facebook or Goodreads. I'll be more than happy to provide you with all the sources I used in my research.

About the Author

Ellie Midwood is a USA Today bestselling and award-winning historical fiction author. She owes her interest in the history of the Second World War to her grandfather, Junior Sergeant in the 2nd Guards Tank Army of the First Belorussian Front, who began telling her about his experiences on the frontline when she was a young girl. Growing up, her interest in history only deepened and transformed from reading about the war to writing about it. After obtaining her BA in Linguistics, Ellie decided to make writing her full-time career and began working on her first full-length historical novel, "The Girl from Berlin." Ellie is continuously enriching her library with new research material and feeds her passion for WWII and Holocaust history by collecting rare memorabilia and documents.

In her free time, Ellie is a health-obsessed yoga

enthusiast, neat freak, adventurer, Nazi Germany history expert, polyglot, philosopher, a proud Jew, and a doggie mama. Ellie lives in New York with her fiancé and their Chihuahua named Shark Bait.

Made in the USA
Coppell, TX
29 July 2020